"My goodness! I have never rea
to Doyle's style- that is, until today, when I discovered this
marvelous book by Hugh Ashton. His 'Watson voice' is impeccable
and so are his interactions between Holmes and Watson."

"The mood captured in the opening of this book was
really perfect. Of course, I am devoted to the Canon,
but I love a good pastiche. The trouble is good pastiches
of the Sherlock stories are hard to come by. I think Mr.
Ashton does an extraordinary job of making me feel like
this could have been part of the original Canon."

"I hardly ever give 5 stars to any Sherlock Holmes
pastiche because I don't believe that anyone can measure
up to the master, A. Conan Doyle, but Hugh Ashton never
disappoints me. His stories are always high quality in the
style, structure and feel of the originals. I have read too many
pastiches to mention and Hugh Ashton's stories would be at
the top of the heap. Do yourself a favor, flop down a couple
bucks and read this entertaining Sherlock Holmes story."

"The Darlington Substitution is an exquisite piece of
writing that does a superb job of recrafting a Holmes tale as
one might read directly from Doyle's unpublished archives.
Given the depth of characters in these stories, and the worldwide
popularity they have achieved, this is a courageous and admirable
feat, successfully managed by a supremely talented writer."

The Darlington Substitution : An Untold Adventure
of Sherlock Holmes
Hugh Ashton

ISBN-13: 978-1-912605-20-0
ISBN-10: 1912605201

Published by j-views Publishing, 2018
© 2012 Hugh Ashton

THE DARLINGTON SUBSTITUTION

CONTENTS

This book is dedicated to Doctor John H. Watson, late of the Indian Army, whose friendship with the great detective Sherlock Holmes, and whose keen eye for description have given the world so much pleasure for so long.

FOREWORD BY
JEFF PEARCE

'VE always remembered a generous comment that John Jakes made about his place in literature, specifically when it came to historical fiction. Jakes is less popular these days, but for quite a while in the 1970s, you could find his paperbacks in every drugstore spin rack and on display tables of every bookshop. He soared up the bestseller charts with chronicles of his Kent family in Revolutionary and Civil War America. Now whatever you might think of his fiction, Jakes at least never gave himself airs, admitting, "Gore Vidal is a Mercedes. I'm a Vega."

His ultimate point was that both will take you where you want to go.

I feel the same way about Hugh Ashton. He has been meticulously building Rolls-Royces for a while now, or if we want to change the metaphor to something more era-appropriate, he's been lovingly restoring a fleet of hansom cabs, all carrying Sherlock and Watson to new stops. He's braver than I am. For my novels, I've been getting by, swiping the odd pony left at a hitching post.

You see, these novels take work. The only thing I've found harder than writing historical fiction is writing history itself, which involves back strain as you hunch over source texts next to your keyboard. You must, quite literally, stop and check for each line that what you're writing is true. Sure, with historical fiction, your hansom cab (or Mercedes, or Vega) must make a hard left and venture into the unconfirmed territory of the imagination. But you better have things plausible when you arrive.

Hugh has proved himself a fan of my alternate history novel, *Reich TV*, but while I researched and checked and double-checked, I still shoehorned certain details to fit my narrative. Not many, mind you, but I did fudge a couple. Technically, that's cheating. You can get away with this for "alternate" history, but even for historical novels, and I've done my share, I will move my chess pieces where I need to and push events a little bit ... that way. My way.

Gore Vidal didn't fudge things—most of the time (and when he did, he admitted it, as he noted in Lincoln or his other novels). And neither does Hugh Ashton. To join him on one of his journeys in late 19th-century Britain is to be enveloped in the smoke of the trains at King's Cross Station and to feel the atmosphere of a grand manor sitting near the harsh and cold country near the Scottish border.

But imagine the double duty of not only trying to capture an historical period, but to capture the voice of one of the most famous and influential authors in the world who wrote in that period? And this is where Hugh's horsepower takes him swiftly past me in the race. I've had fun bringing Josephine Baker back to life, have dug through Paul Robeson's astonishingly powerful and unapologetic blasts to the Red-baiting committee in the U.S. Congress, and I've offered a friendly wave to Hugh in passing as both he and I try to re-animate the most famous Nazi leaders, each of us using them to jump-charge plots of very different books. But could I write in say, Dylan Thomas's style or pour out the lean, scaled-back prose of one of my own favourites, Erich Maria Remarque? Not me, not brave enough. Oh, no, not a chance!

To read *The Case of the Darlington Substitution* is to hear Watson's voice—to rediscover Doyle's style. That's no small feat for any novelist.

And it's an ambitious, possibly even courageous choice. After all, Sherlock has never gone away, not ever. As early as 1899, he was on the New York stage, and we've seen every possible re-imagining of him in books and films ever since, some of which are entertaining and some which are downright awful. We've had Sherlock at the worst of his drug addiction treated by Sigmund Freud. We've had Sherlock meeting Dracula, Sherlock meeting Jack the Ripper, Sherlock as a fool with a smarter Watson, all the way back to Jeremy Brett's stately Holmes on British TV, kept strictly to the Canon.

If you're a fan, like I am, you've gone and sampled many of them. Sitting in the auditorium of the Winnipeg Art Gallery for its weekly film fests, I got to see the old Basil Rathbone films that put Holmes in a modern (well, modern for 1942) Blitzed London. Thirty years later, here we are with Steven Moffatt and Mark Gatiss once again moving our consulting detective to a modern time in the TV show, Sherlock. Take your pick of Sherlocks. You can watch Benedict Cumberbatch, or you can watch Robert Downey Jr. have a go, but frankly, I think of the Guy Ritchie franchise as "Sherlock Lite." Never mind historical accuracy, the two movies in the series barely bother to have our detective do any detecting at all; he's too busy with "buddy banter," action sequence antics and visual gags. Instead of a Vega, we've been whisked off in a go-cart.

This all makes Hugh Ashton's efforts far more rewarding. The pace is how it should be, and from the windows of his hansom cab, the view is more interesting ... and far less blurred. I asked Hugh what he thinks makes his Sherlock stand apart from others.

"I stick very closely to the Canon," he answered simply. "I try to keep Holmes and Watson in character. And I try to have a good reason why the stories were not published before ... I also try to build on the characters of Holmes and Watson. Rather than simply take [Doyle's] characters and jerk them around like marionettes, I try to get into their skin and make them more alive."

I think he's done better than mere re-animation. With Hugh holding the reins, the cab has taken us back to the sitting room in Baker Street, where he's already made sure the furniture is in its old places. Mrs. Hudson knows enough to bring us our tea and telegrams, and instead of a thunderous soundtrack that tells us what to feel in Dolby sound, or even the clever keypad tapping of Benedict Cumberbatch's mobile phone in the BBC series, we have the pleasant and familiar violin of our hero. Here in our cloud of blue pipe-smoke, the room is familiar yet somehow refreshingly new.

And so we've arrived, just in time for a case to unfold. Don't wait on me, go on in. I'll be along in a minute. Hurry now, the game's afoot!

EFF Pearce is the author of close to twenty books, including works of history, current affairs and more than a dozen novels, such as *Reich TV*, *The Karma Booth* and *Bianca: The Silver Age*.

EDITOR'S NOTES

BELIEVED that the deed box containing the untold adventures of Sherlock Holmes as recorded by Dr. Watson had been emptied of all items of interest. Some of the " cases" described therein were little more than lists of names, dates and places, presumably rough jottings for future expanded descriptions.

There were, however, several other cases written out in full, which will require extensive editing before they can be released to the world. Watson appears to have been sadly lacking in concentration when some of these were written. Some paragraphs appear to be missing, some events are described twice in the same adventure, and so on.

As a result, I was about to lay the deed box to one side, after emptying it of all the papers, and removing the small particles of sealing wax and so on which had accumulated within the box. On turning it upside-down to accomplish this, I was astonished when what I had supposed to be the bottom of the box proved to be false, and fell to the ground. A thick envelope had been concealed under it, sealed with the now familiar impressions of the SH and W signet rings, and marked on the front in what I can only assume to be Sherlock Holmes' sprawling, but at the same time splendidly legible, writing, " The Darlington Substitution Case".

Need I say that I was excited by this discovery? Of all of Holmes' cases, there are only four that Watson described at great length, and of those, both *A Study in Scarlet* and *The Valley of Fear* both contain a long digression in which the scene shifts to America. Even *The Sign of Four* contains a lengthy back-story that moves the action outside the main body of the case. I was therefore fully expecting to discover another such tale which, while interesting in its own right, would perhaps not have excited the same attention as a full-length account of a case, such as *The Hound of the Baskervilles*, which focussed its attention on Sherlock Holmes.

The title was, naturally, familiar to me. In the case that Watson entitled " A Scandal in Bohemia" Holmes explains, " In the case of the Darlington substitution scandal, it was of use to me," referring to his claim that the instinct of a woman in the event of a fire is to go to and protect the thing that she values most. It will be remembered that in the former case, he had Watson throw a small incendiary device to " smoke out" (if the pun may be excused) Irene Adler's photograph of the King of Bohemia.

Holmes also employed a deliberately set fire as a device in " The Norwood Builder", and in " A Scandal in Bohemia", he also refers to " the Arnsworth Castle business" where he used the stratagem. Without wishing to accuse Holmes of outright pyromania, it must be admitted that he appeared to have a predilection for this trick, which nonetheless appears to have produced the desired results in most instances.

And in this case, which to my delight I discovered to be concentrated on Holmes, and which sheds new light on his character, as well as that of Watson, the ruse worked once again. The adventure is surely one of the more thrilling of Holmes' exploits, and he finds himself up against one of the most dangerous adversaries in his career. The touch of superstition and sorcery here is in some ways reminiscent of his adventures on Dartmoor in pursuit of the Hound of the Baskervilles, but his opponent is more cunning and dangerous than Stapleton ever proved to be. Holmes, however, is more than a match against his adversary, and holds his own admirably.

Watson, though, has several embarrassing moments that it must have cost him dear to set down, and which are almost certainly the reason for the concealment of this adventure for so long. Once again, we are made almost painfully aware of the double standards of morality in the Victorian era, with the middle class, as represented by Watson, standing for what we now refer to as " Victorian values", and the aristocracy having their own rules, which seem amazingly free and easy, even by today's relaxed standards.

OR those unfamiliar with the British system of nobility and titles, a few words of explanation are necessary. Although the son of a British lord is not a member of the nobility in his own right, he is allowed to use a secondary title of his father, should such a thing exist. His son in turn is permitted to use the third title of his grandfather. In this case, the Earl of Darlington, who was addressed as Lord Darlington, and was also be referred to in that way, also held the title of Baron of Hareby, and his son was therefore addressed and referred to as Lord Hareby. Another title he held was that of Baron of Wittingford, and Hareby's son therefore became Lord Wittingford. The rules are complex, but it appears that Watson has largely followed the correct procedures in his references to the family.

N additional note is necessary with regard to Watson's reporting of the spoken words of those with whom he came in contact. It is to be feared that whatever skills he may have possessed in the relating of the adventures he shared with his friend, and his undoubted expertise in the presentation of the facts appertaining to the cases, John Watson unfortunately appears to have suffered from a " cloth ear" when it comes to reporting speech.

In this particular adventure (and not this one alone), he often appears to have set down the meaning of the words that he heard, rather than the actual words themselves. Occasionally, though, he seems to have added a little phrasing or vocabulary to distinguish speakers of an English that differs from the "standard" middle-class English spoken by Holmes and himself. Even in the latter case related to the major players in these cases, however, it is hard to believe that Holmes or Watson spoke the exact words as recorded here (or in other adventures). The words that Watson put into the mouths of those characters featured in his accounts who hail from other regions or social classes are likewise often somewhat unlikely.

Even so, there is a certain charm attached to Watson's rendition of the speech of the characters in the adventures he describes, and it would be presumptuous of me to attempt any changes to this. As Holmes remarks in The Lion's Mane, " how much he [Watson] might have made of such a wonderful happening and my eventual triumph", showing that Holmes himself, however much he may have deprecated Watson's sensational accounts of his (Holmes') exploits, was not immune to the spells that his friend's narratives could cast over those who read them.

Hugh Ashton
Kamakura, 2012

THE DARLINGTON SUBSTITUTION

AN UNTOLD ADVENTURE OF SHERLOCK HOLMES

DISCOVERED AND EDITED BY

HUGH ASHTON

J-VIEWS PUBLISHING, LICHFIELD, ENGLAND

THE MACE OF
SUCCESSION

Chapter I

Lord Darlington
of Hareby Hall

F all the adventures I experienced with my friend Sherlock Holmes, one of the most intriguing was that in which we found ourselves involved at the behest of the late Earl of Darlington.

Holmes had recently returned from a visit to the Continent, about which he remained close-lipped, which in my experience betokened a commission executed for some powerful patron, when Mrs. Hudson brought up a telegram.

" It's reply-paid, sir," she said to Holmes. " Will there be an answer ? " She waited patiently as Holmes ripped open the envelope and perused the contents.

" There will be an answer, Mrs. Hudson," he informed her, scribbling a few words on a sheet of notepaper and handing it to her. " Thank you."

"What was that ? " I asked, as our landlady made her way downstairs. " Are you at liberty to provide me with details ? "

" I suppose that I am free to tell you all I know of the business, which is virtually nothing." He passed the telegram over to me, and I read the words, "WISH TO RETAIN YOUR SERVICES ON BIZARRE MATTER. TRAGIC CONSEQUENCES IF MISHANDLED. ALFRED DARLINGTON."

" The use of the term 'bizarre' within a telegraphic communication is in itself somewhat bizarre, I feel," I commented. " What was your answer ? "

He smiled. " How could I resist such an appeal ? Naturally, I accepted. The reply was addressed to his club, so I would expect to see him here in person in a very short space of time."

" Have you no ideas regarding this ? "

" None," he replied simply. " The Earl is one of the most respected members of the House of Lords. He has served with distinction in several Cabinets, and I can recall no breath of scandal or anything that could reflect adversely on him, other than that unfortunate affair some years ago, where I was able to exonerate his distant cousin, who had been accused of some peculation involving the funds of a company of which he was director. That was too commonplace to be termed bizarre, and I would hardly foresee tragic consequences arising from it. Have you any knowledge of his family or his background?" Holmes asked me. "I know that you follow these society matters closer than do I."

"His immediate family consists of merely the one son, considerably younger than himself—he married late in life, and his wife died in childbirth. The son, Lord Hareby, married about eighteen months back. It was a fashionable wedding—the talk of the town."

"The news would appear to have passed me by," commented Holmes drily. "Though Hareby was a member of my College at University, we hardly ever passed the time of day. We had little in common."

He picked up his violin and started to saw away at it, producing a melody that was, to my ears, not untuneful, but slightly discordant at times. When he had finished, I asked him the name of the composer, and was astounded to be informed that this was one of Holmes' own improvisations. Though I could never claim to be any kind of expert in the field, it would seem that music lost a composer of some talent when Sherlock Holmes turned his attention to crime.

A ring at the front door announced the arrival of a visitor, and there was soon a knock at the door of our rooms. A liveried footman stood without, who bowed slightly to Holmes as he opened the door.

"Lord Darlington requests that Mr. Sherlock Holmes and Dr. John Watson join him for luncheon at his club, since his lordship's gout is troubling him, making it difficult for him to make a visit in person," he announced.

"We are pleased to accept his lordship's invitation," replied Holmes. "We will be with him presently."

The servant coughed. " His lordship has dispatched his carriage, which is waiting in the street. I was asked to inform you that there is no need for formality. His lordship's words to you were, 'Please come as you are and do not trouble yourself overly about your appearance or dress.'"

" That is most kind of him," replied Holmes.

In a few minutes, we were seated in the Darlington carriage, which drew up outside the Athenaeum Club.

" His Lordship informed me that he would be waiting for you in the library," the footman informed us as he held open the door to allow us to alight.

It was the first time that I had entered the hallowed precincts of the Athenaeum, and I looked about me with interest, but it seemed that Holmes was quite accustomed to the place, and strode across the entrance hall, hardly acknowledging the welcome of the porter.

The Earl of Darlington was seated in a chair near the door of the library, and half rose in his place as Holmes and I entered the room, but Holmes motioned to him to keep his seat.

" Please do not trouble yourself," Holmes assured him. " Your man informed us that you were suffering from gout. My sincere sympathy."

" Thank you, Holmes," replied the Earl. " It is a confounded nuisance, to say the least, but I trust it is not too much of an inconvenience for you to come here. Please take a seat, and you, too, Dr. Watson. Might I trouble you to speak up a little ? I suffer somewhat from deafness. Age creeps on, and the result of my service in the Navy as a gunnery officer has also afflicted me, I fear."

We seated ourselves in armchairs facing the elderly nobleman, whose white hair framing a lined, but honest, countenance, told of a life well spent in the service of his country. He called for two glasses of sherry for Holmes and myself, contenting himself with a glass of water. " All that the medicos will allow me these days before a meal nowadays, Watson," he told me. "What is your prescription for your patients in my condition?"

"Much the same, I fear, sir."

He sighed. "I suppose it was too much to expect a second opinion with which I could find agreement," he answered, with a somewhat roguish grin. "But before luncheon, let me advise you more fully of the matter." The Earl turned to Holmes and spoke more gravely. "I should warn you that what I am about to say may seem almost fantastical, but I would ask you to hear me out before passing judgement."

"I will endeavour to keep an open mind," replied Holmes, stretching out his long legs, and adopting an attitude that appeared somnolent, but betokened, as I knew from past experience, the utmost in mental attention.

HE peer proceeded with his speech. "The whole matter started some three hundred and fifty years ago and is recorded in an ancient manuscript to be found in the library of our Hall at Hareby in Northumberland. One of my ancestors, a certain Edward, the second of our line to bear the title of Earl, was constantly engaged in one of the countless border skirmishes against the Scots, who were, as you will remember, ruled by their own monarch at that time, having yet to come under the rule of England. This was, of course, not a formal war declared by sovereigns against each other, but, to speak frankly, was more in the nature of brigandage carried out by gangs of robbers on both sides. In one of these raids, one of those captured from Scotland was an old woman, shunned by her own folk as a witch, and a bringer of bad luck to those who crossed her path. My ancestor laughed at this superstition, as he termed it, and scorned those who feared the woman as a witch.

" Indeed, so little did he heed this belief that he took to inviting the woman, whose name is recorded as Margaret Harris, and sometimes is referred to in the records as 'Mad Maggie', to share his table in the Hall, though whether this was done in a spirit of bravado to show his contempt for the beliefs of others, or as an act of mockery against the poor woman, is uncertain.

" One night, Edward, who is reported to have been drinking deeply, challenged Mad Maggie to demonstrate her powers of witchcraft. For answer, she withdrew from her clothing a curious wooden object, apparently fashioned from the twisted root of a hawthorn tree.

" 'Mark ye this,' she croaked. 'This is the Mace of Succession, and mark ye well its purpose.'

" 'And its purpose is what, old woman?' mocked my ancestor.

" 'See ye here,' she replied to him. 'In the head of the Mace are set eleven silver pennies, each marking a generation from now. When your first-born son comes to be born' (for at that time Edward was unmarried and had no heir) 'within seven days of his birth, ere he be christened, then must ye remove one of the pennies from the Mace and throw it down the well that stands in the courtyard. When his heir is born, then do ye remove the next penny and do the same. And for his son, the same, until all the pennies be gone.'

" 'And then?' asked Edward of the crone, still mocking her.

" 'Then will your line come to an end.' A hush fell over the assembly at these words, which were uttered in a tone of finality.

" 'And if we should fail to do this thing at the birth of an heir?' asked Edward, much of his mockery now gone.

" 'Then will the new-born die," replied Mad Maggie simply. 'His head will be crushed by the Mace. You and yours cannot escape the doom I have laid upon your line. One generation shall live for every month that ye have held me captive and made sport of me. For nearly a year ye have done these things to me, but tonight is my last night of life, and I present the Mace to ye as my final act upon this earth.' So saying, she handed the curious knobbed root with its burden of silver pennies to Edward, and seated herself at the table opposite to him, staring at him with a fixed glare, and making no answer to his queries, which became more and more enraged as she sat silently facing him. At length, wearying of her silent obstinacy, he fetched a blow to the side of her head. Mad Maggie slipped to the ground, lifeless, and it was then obvious to all that her silence had not been the result of obstinacy, but of death.

" So far, Mr. Holmes, the story has contained nothing of the unnatural, though it is certainly an unusual and macabre tale. But now comes the report of an event which I, as a rational modern man, can hardly credit, but is recorded in the same vein of sober fact as the rest.

" Edward, shaken by the words of the old woman, and by her sudden demise, gave a hoarse laugh. 'Am I a foolish peasant to be moved by the words of an old woman such as that, and to be frightened by a stick?' He seized the Mace, as it had been termed by the hag, and flung it into the fire. As the stick touched the flame, there was a loud report, and burning logs from the fireplace were scattered about the room, causing those in the hall hurriedly to douse the number of small fires that were thereby started. As for the Mace itself, it lay alone in the middle of the fireplace ; all other coals and wood there having been dispersed by the explosion. I notice your scepticism, and am merely reporting the events as described in the chronicle, Mr. Holmes."

" Your story is most interesting," replied Holmes, " to antiquarians who collect such tales. However, there would appear to be some sort of prophecy involved that has a relevance to the present day. If there were to be eleven generations from that date, when will the eleventh be?"

"That is the heart of the matter, Mr. Holmes. My son is the tenth generation. His wife is now with child, their first, and should the child be a boy, he will be the eleventh heir, and the last of the line. There is now but one silver penny in the head of the Mace."

"Could you not simply ignore the ritual, and leave the coin where it is?" I asked.

The Earl turned his gaze towards me. "Would that we could," he replied sorrowfully. "Believe me, there have been attempts in the past to cheat the prophecy. The sixth Earl, my great-grandfather, believing no more in these matters than he would in the existence of a mermaid, for example, declined to follow the custom. The morning after he announced his decision to do this, his new-born son was found dead. He had apparently slipped from his cradle, and had fallen on his head, crushing his skull. There is a similar family tradition, though it is not recorded in writing, regarding the third Earl, Edward's son, and his first-born boy, who likewise died in a fall from his crib following his father's refusal to perform the ritual. Since my great-grandfather's time, our family has felt it expedient to follow the ceremony as laid down by Mad Maggie. Though, as I say, I consider myself a rational man, I nonetheless would not care to abandon the custom."

"Could you not simply dispose of the Mace?" enquired Holmes. "No, I see by your face that the idea is unthinkable to you. I see. I fail, however, to understand exactly what it is that you require of me."

"The problem, Mr. Holmes," replied the other, "is that the Mace has disappeared."

"And when is the birth of your grandchild expected?" asked Holmes. "Forgive my indelicacy in asking this question, but it is important to know these things if I am to take any action in this case. It would seem that there is some sort of restriction with regard to time here."

The peer flushed a little, but answered, " I believe that the blessed event is due within the month. Naturally, we do not know whether it will prove to be a male heir, but should it transpire to be so, we should expect to complete the Ritual of the Mace. It would be a sorrowful event, because according to the prophecy, the next male heir would be the last. And it would be even more sorrowful, if the old tales are true, if we were to omit this, as it would result in the death of the heir."

" Surely, you as a modern man of a rational age, cannot seriously believe this ancient superstition ? " I burst out.

The Earl seemed a little astounded at the temerity of my statement, but answered me courteously enough. " Dr. Watson, I could quote the old saw about there being more things in heaven and earth and so on, but your question deserves more than that glib answer. My answer is that although I do not believe in the literal truth of Mad Maggie's prophecy, I do not disbelieve it either—at least, not to the extent that I wish to disregard it. I may add that my son entertains a much firmer belief in the old tales than do I."

" And his wife ? "

" She laughs at the whole business, and refuses to take it at all seriously."

" So my brief," Holmes broke in, " is to recover the Mace, and to hope with all my heart that I find it. Alternatively, in the event of my failing to retrieve the missing artefact, I should be hoping with all my might that your daughter-in-law is delivered of a baby girl."

" That would seem to sum up the situation admirably, Mr. Holmes. I take it from that you are prepared to serve me in this matter ? "

" There are one or two trifling affairs that must be cleared up before I can make the trip to Northumberland, but you make take it for the moment that I will assist you. I would be grateful, however, if you could provide me with more information regarding the disappearance of the Mace."

"With pleasure," replied the Earl. "Shall we adjourn to luncheon? I assume you have no objection to discussing the matter while we eat?" On receiving the required reassurance from Holmes, he summoned a club servant, who assisted him into the dining-room, Holmes and myself following.

"You must understand," he began, between the oysters that formed the first part of our meal, "that despite the title I bear, and my reputed wealth, I live a relatively simple life. The staff at Hareby Hall are few in number, and have been with me for years. I often protest to them that they deserve more in the way of wages than I currently pay them, but they are content to stay on, claiming that they are used to the Hall, and to my family and myself. Bouverie, the butler, is the chief of the indoor servants, and he is supported by his wife who acts as housekeeper. They entered my service some thirty years or more. The cook is assisted by two kitchen-maids, and Mrs. Bouverie supervises the activities of a parlour-maid and three housemaids. Believe me, given the size of the Hall, this is a modest establishment. The outside staff consists of three grooms who also act as coachmen, and a head gardener who employs local lads as the seasons demand. To be frank, the grounds are somewhat of a wilderness, a state that I prefer to an over-manicured and artificial garden. Ah, the salmon," he broke off, as the waiters brought our next course. "It is truly excellent here."

He ceased to speak for a few minutes, presumably to show his appreciation of the fish dish, which was, as he had claimed, of a surpassing delicacy. "To continue," he said at length, after having wiped his lips with his napkin. "The Mace is kept with what little jewellery remains in the family, following the depredations caused by the sixth Earl's losses at faro, in a strong metal cabinet that is set into the wall in my library—a sort of ancient safe. I must confess that I hardly ever have call to open the cabinet, and before I opened it a few days ago the last time that I recollect doing so was over three months previously. The cabinet is kept locked, and I am the sole possessor of the only key in the household. As it happens, there is one other key, but I prefer to keep that in a safety deposit box at my bank. As I say, there is very little occasion for me to open the cabinet.

" Imagine my surprise, Mr. Holmes, when I opened the cabinet the other day and discovered it to be completely empty. The Mace had disappeared and so had all the jewellery. The cupboard was bare, as the old children's rhyme has it."

" Excuse me," interrupted my friend, " can you please explain to me why you opened the cabinet at all, given that your future grandchild is not imminently expected? "

" That is a very good point, Mr. Holmes," replied the peer. " The cabinet makes a most distinctive sound when it is closed, a kind of metallic ringing sound, which is totally unlike any other sound in the house. I fancied I heard that sound two nights ago as I lay in bed. As I mentioned earlier, though, I am more than a little deaf, and I could not be positive that I had heard correctly. The next morning, I resolved to investigate, in the event that my ears had not been playing me false."

" Do you sleep close to the room containing the cabinet? " enquired Holmes, who by now had brought out his notebook and was making notes.

" The room in which I sleep is on the ground floor, next to the library," replied the Earl. " My gout prevents me from occupying apartments where I must climb stairs to reach them."

" So there is no doubt in your mind that the noise you heard was the cabinet door being closed? "

" None. None, that is, unless I were dreaming, which I

confess was my first thought. Ah, the saddle of lamb. My doctors forbid it, and my palate is far from being what it once was, but I would be obliged if you gentlemen would partake of the club claret. We have a particularly fine Mouton-Rothschild in the cellars that I think you will enjoy." He summoned a waiter and gave appropriate instructions. "Now, where was I? Ah, yes. I did believe it was a dream until I woke in the morning, and made my way to the library, still in my dressing-gown, and opened the cabinet. It was a shock to see it empty, I can assure you of that."

"What did you do upon your discovery?" asked Holmes. "I assume you raised the alarm?"

"I did not," replied the peer. "The jewellery is insured, for an amount that is probably above its real value, and it is in any case hideous to my eyes. We are well rid of it, if my honest opinion is to be sought. However, it was the Mace that was the true loss. Although it is no more than a tree root, and contains but one silver penny, it is, to my mind, one of the few things," and here he lowered his voice to little more than a whisper, so that we had to strain to catch his meaning, "one of the few things that saves my poor son from total lunacy."

I stared at him, horror-struck, and Holmes, who had been scribbling in his notebook, stopped his writing. At that moment the waiter brought our wine, and conversation lapsed.

"Excuse me," said Holmes, when the waiter had departed. "I had the honour of knowing your son slightly at University. We are of an age, though our interests differed, and though I would never claim to have known him well, he had nothing of that nature about him then."

"Ah, it is a sad case," replied the Earl, wagging his head. "The poor lad was, as you might recall, a sportsman. One of his chief delights lay in fox-hunting, and one day while engaged in this pursuit, he was thrown from his horse, and his head was dashed against a large stone. Though the physical injury soon healed, it was obvious that something had been damaged in his mind. While before the accident he had shown a tendency towards superstition, now it has become an obsession with him. As in many stables, the grooms keep cats to help rid the place of mice, and some of the cats that they kept until recently were black. My son one day went to the stables and ordered the grooms and stable lads to dispose of the offending felines in any way they saw fit. Since then, there are no stable cats, and there are none in the house."

"I see," said Holmes. "This certainly is unfortunate. Are there any other instances of this?"

The Earl sighed. "Indeed there are. Pray, do partake of your wine, both of you, if my conversation is not spoiling your appetite."

I sipped the noble beverage and it was, indeed, of a quality such as I had seldom encountered, though as his Lordship had intimated, my palate was somewhat blunted by the disturbing tales we were hearing.

"Yes, indeed," continued our host. "The old superstition about spilled salt seems to have been taken to heart in his case. Usually, the custom after spilling salt is to throw a pinch over one's left shoulder, is it not?" This was addressed to me, and I nodded in agreement. "Well, in the case of my son, this has been taken to extremes. Not only does he throw the salt over his shoulder, but this ritual is preceded by his rising and circling the table three times in an anti-clockwise direction." He sighed. "There are other similar superstitions that he continues to observe, but I will not bore you with them."

"And these superstitions include the Mace?" asked Holmes.

"Indeed they do. Though he has hardly ever seen the Mace, except on those rare occasions when I have opened the cabinet to allow his wife to wear the jewels to a social occasion, hardly a day seems to pass without his mentioning it."

" But he does not express a wish to see it ? " asked Holmes.

" He merely wishes to be satisfied that it is in a safe place, it seems. But it preys on his mind, especially since his wife, er ... discovered that she was to be delivered of a child." His voice tailed off into a discreet silence. " I fear that he would become totally deranged were he to discover that the Mace was missing. He has become overly sensitive to such matters. There was a time when he was as manly a young person as one could ever hope to meet. Now," he shook his head sadly, " he weeps at the smallest thing and can become quite inconsolable over such accidents as the discovery of a dead sparrow. His moods of elation are just as sudden. This confounded hunting fall has completely disturbed the balance of his mind."

" When did this unfortunate hunting accident take place ? " asked Holmes.

" A little less than nine months ago."

" And his wife's reaction ? "

" She gives the appearance of being a most solicitous spouse," replied the Earl. " She sympathises with him and humours him in his fancies. I take this to be deleterious to his mental state, but she will not be dissuaded.""

" Pardon my intrusion into your family affairs," said Holmes, " but could you tell me whether their bed-rooms are close to yours ? "

" They occupy two adjacent apartments, separated by a common bathroom, at the other end of the wing from the room where I sleep, and on the second floor," replied the other, obviously somewhat puzzled by Holmes' query.

" Thank you. Now if we may return to the question of the cabinet and the missing Mace. Where do you keep your key ? "

" It is on my watch-chain here. You may see it here," displaying a large key of the Bramah pattern. " It never leaves my chain."

" But your chain must leave your person sometimes," pointed out Holmes.

" When I am asleep or bathing, naturally. On the other hand, I am a light sleeper, as a result of this confounded gout, and I am certain that I would be awakened if there was an attempt made to remove the key from my side."

" Very good. Let us return to the subject of the Mace itself. Can you provide us with a description ? "

" It is, as I mentioned, a curiously twisted root of the hawthorn tree, a little over two feet in length, with a curious knobbed end. In that end there is one silver penny and ten slits into which the previous generations' pennies were inserted. The penny is blackened by tarnish, and would not be instantly recognised as a coin by any person who had no knowledge of the artefact. I can see no reason for any thief to take it."

" How many people knew of its disappearance and its significance ? " enquired Holmes.

" My son, his wife and myself. This is not something that we wish to be noised abroad, as you can imagine. The story itself is no secret, of course. The manuscript describing Earl Edward and Mad Maggie is kept in the library, in the family records, so it is possible that one of the servants, for instance, Bouverie, could have chanced upon it and read through the family history, but frankly, I see that as being unlikely, and there would be no reason for him to take the Mace. In any event, he would not know where the Mace was secreted. The cabinet is let into the wall of the library, and is usually hidden by a portrait—ironically, that of the third Earl Edward, with whom this whole business began."

" So you would wish me to investigate ? I shall be ready to do that in a few days. There are one or two trifling matters that I would like to see completed before I set myself on the trail of your mystery. In the meantime, I am sure that Watson here will have no objection to travelling to Hareby Hall for one or two nights until I arrive."

It was a very thinly disguised hint, which I took, accepting the Earl's hospitality.

" Excellent," said he. " I shall be taking the night sleeper to Berwick from King's Cross this evening. Shall I ask my man to reserve you a berth on the same train ? "

" With pleasure," I replied.

" And now," said Holmes, " maybe we should talk of different matters. May I ask your opinion on the Balkan situation, sir ? Are the Serbs justified, in your opinion, in seeking their independence from Vienna ? "

The meal passed pleasantly enough, and we parted from Lord Darlington, after he and I had made arrangements for our meeting at the station later.

ELL, and what do you make of that pretty little puzzle ? " asked Holmes, as we strolled back to Baker-street.

" I am in the dark," I confessed. " First of all, it is a mystery to me how such a man as the Earl can believe in that superstitious nonsense, reminding me of nothing so much as the balderdash we used to hear in India."

" Maybe I am more tolerant of such things than are you," replied Holmes.

I stared at him. " My dear Holmes, are you telling me that you too are a subscriber to this ridiculous rigmarole ? "

" By no means," he replied. " Let me explain. When I say that I am tolerant of such things, I do not mean that I myself believe in them. Rather that I find them as absurd as do you, but I am more tolerant of those who do find some comfort in them."

" What possible comfort can anyone find in the story of a

piece of wood that is believed to kill the heirs to the line?" I retorted. "I can understand that some of these tales may provide some sort of solace, but this one really does not seem to fall under that heading."

"The comfort in this one, Watson, lies in the fact that his family is considered important and significant enough to suffer under a curse. The Curse of the Harebys has a certain ring to it, do you not think? The phrase 'the Curse of the Watsons' lacks the same majestic note, I feel."

Despite myself, I laughed at Holmes' idea. "As far as I know, none of my ancestors has ever suffered in that way. I suppose there is some truth in what you say."

"I know it to be the simple truth," replied Holmes. "A family haunting or a curse lifts the clan in the eyes of others."

"How long will I be at Hareby waiting for you, and what do you wish me to do there?"

"There are several things that I wish of you," replied my friend. "First, I wish you to act as a companion to our friend who has just provided us with lunch. From his description, he is a lonely man, and his son and his wife would appear to provide little comfort. Endeavour to raise his spirits, if you can. He is sociable by nature, it would seem, and lacks the opportunity to talk and converse as he would wish. I am fearful that he may fall into some sort of decline if he is on his own, and the consequences of his illness and death could indeed be serious. That is your first task."

"There are others?"

"Indeed there are. As a doctor, even though you have not specialised in nervous diseases, your opinions regarding the eccentricities of the heir would be most welcome. Observe and note all that you can in that area, and it will be of great value to me."

"And what of the wife?"

"There you have a conundrum. The Earl hardly spoke of

her, did he? I wish you to observe what sort of relations obtain between the three major players in this little drama: the Earl, his son, and his son's wife."

"You believe there to be no-one of significance in this drama outside those three?"

"It is possible there will be other players, but if so, they will not be at Hareby. They are more likely to be here in London, where I will be for the next few days. I would highly appreciate it, Watson, if you would send me regular reports from Hareby."

"Regarding what?"

"You know my methods. Write to me regarding anything that, in your opinion, will help me deduce the solution to this case. You are to send a telegram if possible, but I know that in rural areas the post-office may be at some distance, and in those cases the regular postal service will have to suffice. I would advise, by the way, packing your doctor's bag and its accoutrements."

"Why?" I asked in some surprise.

"I rather anticipate that your skills as a physician may be in demand."

"By the Earl? Or by his son?"

"Either. Or both. Or possibly by another," he replied, enigmatically. "Also," he remarked, after a silence of some minutes, "I feel that adding your Army revolver and some ammunition to your luggage would not come amiss."

"You have suspicions already?"

"I have inklings, Watson. Mere inklings as yet, and though some would write these off as being merely irrational fancies, I am sufficiently in touch with my inner self to realise that these are the result of rational thoughts that have yet to find their full expression. I fear we are dealing with some dark forces, and I do not refer to any supernatural agency here, but rather the evil that lurks in the hearts of human beings."

CHAPTER II
HAREBY HALL

T was therefore with some trepidation that I packed for the journey, including those items that Holmes had recommended to me. I reached King's Cross Station at the time that the Earl and I had appointed, and discovered him waiting for me.

"Ah, good. First-class sleeping berths have been secured for the two of us. Have you eaten dinner?"

I assured him that I had.

"I too. But perhaps you will join me for a nightcap before retiring?" I remembered Holmes' thoughts about this elderly man and his possible feelings of solitude, and accepted the invitation.

As the train pulled out of the station, we sat companionably in the dining car over our drinks, chatting of this and that. At length, he yawned mightily.

"Forgive me," he apologised to me. "As an older man, I need my sleep."

I reassured him that I too needed my rest, and that he was not inconveniencing me by his retiring.

The sleeping compartment that had been reserved for me was comfortable, and I drifted off to sleep, to be woken early the next morning by the train attendant, knocking on the compartment door to inform me that the train would arrive at Berwick in about thirty minutes. I rose and dressed, but omitted much of my toilet, since I had no wish to shave on a moving train, hoping that the Earl would likewise omit this procedure and that I could make myself presentable when we reached Hareby.

As we pulled into Berwick, we left our compartments at almost the same time, and greeted each other in the corridor.

"A little colder than London," he observed, pulling his travelling coat around him. Indeed, there was a distinct nip in the early morning air. The sun had only just risen, and the morning mist had yet to disperse as we stepped onto the platform.

"Ah, Hanshaw," commented the Earl to a red-faced tweed-clad man of about sixty years of age who met us and touched his cap in greeting. "Thank you," as our baggage was loaded onto a porter's trolley. "This is Doctor Watson," indicating me, "who will be staying with us for a few days."

"Pleased to make your acquaintance, sir," replied the coachman. "It's a raw morning, sir," he addressed Lord Darlington. "I've placed the travelling rugs and I'll be putting some hot-water bottles in the trap. If you'll excuse me, I'll just go and get some hot water from the refreshment room for the hot-water bottles. That is, sir, if you don't want to stop for a cup of tea there before we set off for the Hall." His manner, while respectful of the Earl's position, was nonetheless cordial, and bespoke a genuine affection for his elderly master. He spoke with the local accent which, though at times difficult to understand, nonetheless recalled to me my service with the Fifth Northumberland Fusiliers where the dialect and everyday speech of the barrack-room resembled that which I was now hearing.

"Thank you, Hanshaw. That is most thoughtful of you," replied Lord Darlington. "Watson, what say you to the idea of a cup of tea before our departure from here? It is approximately forty minutes' drive from here to the Hall."

"Begging your pardon, sir, but it's closer to an hour's journey today. The rains of the past few days have washed away the bridge near Blythedale," commented his servant.

"In which case, a spot of tea is definitely called for. Please join us at our table when you have finished your preparations, Hanshaw."

We moved into the comparative warmth of the station refreshment room, where the Earl was recognised and greeted by the staff, and a steaming pot of tea was set before us. I could

not refrain from asking my companion about his previous invitation to his servant to join us.

"Hanshaw's a good man," he replied. "I don't want to see
him shivering with cold as he drives us home, when I could so
easily make his life more comfortable. In any event, he is my
window onto the estate. He knows everybody and everything
in the area, and I can find out more about the way things
are going in five minutes by talking to him than I could find
out by myself in five days. Quite frankly, outside London, I
have very few concerns about the rank or station of those with
whom I converse. In Town, of course, it is a somewhat different matter. One has a position to keep up."

Sure enough, Hanshaw joined us in a short while, and he
and Lord Darlington were soon engaged in conversation about
people and places of which I had no knowledge. The conversation on both sides was cordial and courteous—the Earl obviously respectful of the knowledge of his servant, who in his
turn showed the due regard for his master's rank that I had
previously remarked. I was amused to see the peer's usually
aristocratic speech take on some of the local colour as he conversed with the coachman.

At length the conversation between master and man came
to an end, and we set off for the Hall in the trap. The sun had
now risen, and the morning mist had burned off. The rugged
countryside of dales and becks, with the Cheviot Hills forming
a backdrop, formed a deep impression on me, and I mentioned
the lonely aspect of the countryside to my host.

"Yes indeed, it is a wild landscape," said he. "One can
well imagine the moss troopers sweeping down from the north
and carrying off cattle, and the redcoats vainly trying to stop
their depredations."

"Or your ancestor making his raids to the Scottish border,"
I ventured, "and carrying off Mad Maggie."

"Yes," he said shortly. It was obvious to me that he had no

wish to pursue the subject further, and I held my tongue on the matter, choosing instead, after several minutes had passed, to enquire after the peculiarities of the Cheviot sheep dotting the green fields with specks of white, with rough stone walls marking the boundaries between fields. There were few other signs of human habitation, other than scattered hamlets, often consisting of no more than three or four houses huddled together, as if for shelter from the cold winds that sweep across the high expanses of the moors.

While conversing on such bucolic matters, we turned into the drive leading to the Hall, which I now beheld for the first time. A once-handsome building that I judged to have been built in the late Elizabethan or early Jacobean era, it had suffered from the ravages of time, as well as those of well-meaning architects, who had tacked on undoubtedly practical, but at the same time discordant, additions to the building. The whole effect was now decidedly unbalanced to my eyes, and was not altogether pleasing.

However, this did not impress itself upon me nearly so much as did the change in my companion's countenance. While up to this time he had been cheerful enough, as he caught sight of the Hall, his face seemed to fall, and his spirit seemed to shrink, almost visibly.

I could only ascribe this sudden change in his spirits to the thought of his son, once a healthy young man, and now bogey-ridden and childlike, who would inherit the place, and decided to hold my peace about the subject.

HE trap drew up outside the front door of the Hall, which was opened from within.

" Ah, Bouverie," remarked the Earl, his spirits apparently somewhat lifted by the sight of the retainer. " It is good to be back again."

" And always a pleasure for us to see you back here, sir," replied the butler. I was pleased to see that the same spirit of easy camaraderie with their master, mingled with respect, was shared by both Hanshaw and Bouverie. I was intrigued by this attitude, which was somewhat at odds with the rather conservative politics that had been displayed by the Earl in the Cabinet post that he had held some years previously.

" Is Lord Hareby here ? " the Earl asked.

" No, sir, he is walking in the park. He went out immediately after breakfast."

" And Lady Hareby ? "

" She felt unwell, and retired to her room."

Lord Darlington sighed. " Well, Watson," he said to me, " it looks as though we will make our breakfast à deux, if that does not displease you too much ? "

I readily agreed, adding, " However, before we eat, I would very much appreciate a chance to shave and so on, if that is possible."

" My dear chap ! " He was instantly solicitousness itself. " Unpardonable of me. Bouverie, please show Doctor Watson to his room, and ensure that he has everything he needs to be comfortable. How long will you require ? " he asked me.

" No more than twenty minutes, I would guess."

" Excellent. I shall see you then," he answered.

I was shown to a charming room which apparently formed part of the original fabric of the house. My bed was an antique carved oak four-poster, obviously several hundred years old, and the other furnishings were in keeping.

" I will bring you your hot water in a few minutes, sir," the butler informed me.

When he had brought it, I thanked him, and waited for him to leave me. However, he seemed reluctant to depart, and I asked him if everything was in order.

" Yes, sir. I have no worries. It is only that I want to let you know, sir ... " He hesitated.

" Well, what is it ? "

" If you are to hear any crying, or weeping, or sounds of that nature coming from down the passageway, sir, please ignore them." He hesitated again, and I motioned for him to continue. " His young lordship is not well. There are times when the poor young man does not seem able to keep himself from weeping for hours on end. If you'll pardon the liberty, sir, I would not advise going near him in that state. He has been known to say and do things that are somewhat unsocial in their nature."

" For example ? " I asked.

" There was one time, sir, when he became somewhat distraught about a ladder that had been placed against the wall for the purpose of cleaning the windows. Somehow he had failed to notice that he had walked under it, and being subject to these fancies and beliefs, was under the impression that some sort of bad luck would befall him. He began to worry about it and started to weep, and my wife, who is housekeeper here, and has known him since he was a lad, went up to him to try to comfort him. He would have none of it, and thrust her away so roughly that she fell over onto the ground. He took no notice of her, and walked on. It seemed that he had no knowledge of what he had done."

Some sort of comment seemed to be called for at this point. " Dear, dear," I remarked. " And when this fit of depression had passed ? "

" After he'd stopped crying, sir, he was as nice as could be to her. He said he was sorry, and started to cry again. There's no harm in him, sir, but since that fall he's been a bit … "

" I understand," I replied, not wishing to embarrass him further by forcing him to put a name to the unfortunate man's condition. " As it happens, I am a doctor of medicine, and I have some experience with patients of this kind." In actual fact, I had relatively little experience with nervous cases, but I had kept up to date with the available literature, and one of my brother officers in India had suffered from a malady whose symptoms sounded similar to those described by Bouverie.

" That's a relief, sir," replied the butler. " If you can make him better, we'll all be most grateful to you." Obviously he was under the impression that my purpose in visiting Hareby was to cure the poor man of his ills.

" There are limits to what can be achieved," I replied, as noncommittally as I could manage. " In the meantime, thank you for the information." He bowed and left me pondering what had just been told to me.

Breakfast with the Earl was a somewhat gloomy affair. My host seemed somewhat sunk in his own thoughts, and I had little wish to break in on whatever business was occupying his mind. However, as the almost silent meal drew to an end, he turned to me with a friendly smile and asked me if I was interested in taking a shotgun around the estate.

" I am sorry, but pressure of business prevents my accompanying you," he apologised to me, but you are welcome to make your own way along the dale."

" If I might forego the gun," I replied, " I would enjoy the walk."

So saying, in thirty minutes I was suitably equipped for a day to be spent walking in the countryside, with a packet of sandwiches provided through the graces of Mrs. Bouverie.

What happened next is best told in the words of the report I wrote and transmitted to Sherlock Holmes later that day, the latter part of which I quote here.

Chapter III

From the first report of John H. Watson to Sherlock Holmes

OMIT the first part of my report to Holmes, which told of the journey to Hareby as I have described it earlier.

" ... *I set off from the Hall, having obtained an Ordnance Survey map of the surroundings from Bouverie, the butler. I had covered, according to the map, a distance of just over one mile, when I heard a low keening sound, somewhat unearthly in nature, emanating from a small copse about twenty yards from my current position.*

" Though I had no idea what the noise might be, and I was, naturally, unarmed other than for a stout walking stick, for I had left my revolver in the Hall, I decided to investigate, and struck out for the copse.

" Much to my surprise, I discovered a well-dressed man, whom I took to be Lord Hareby, kneeling on the ground, staring intently at some object in front of him, and making the hideous groans that had originally attracted my attention. Mindful of the warning regarding violence that had been imparted to me earlier by Bouverie, I moved to a position where I was clearly visible to him, should he care to lift his gaze, judging that he, like certain wild animals, might be ready to strike at those who surprised him, and might, if aware of an intruder, tolerate its presence.

" When I had reached the spot in question, I coughed gently in an attempt to attract his attention. There was no effect, so I spoke in as gentle a voice as I could manage. 'Can I help you?' I asked him. I noted the object of his gaze—a dead sparrow.

" He did not answer with words, but acknowledged my presence by ceasing his moaning, and lifting his head to stare at me. The eyes were vacant of expression—nay, even of intelligence. When we look into a dog's eyes we see intelligence and character, but this was something entirely different—there was no sign of humanity in that gaze. My blood was chilled, but I stood quiet and still, waiting for some response. At length he spoke slowly in a voice that was devoid of all expression.

" 'Thank you, but I require nothing,' were his words, spoken in a voice that spoke of education and breeding while at the same time being, as I said, expressionless. The effect was peculiarly horrible, and reminded me of nothing so much as the voices of unfortunate madmen that I had once heard as a medical student on a visit to the lunatic asylum.

" 'You must be cold,' I said to him. 'Let me lend you my coat.' Though it was not in actual fact cold, my thought was that the sensation of human touch would increase his awareness of me as another human being, and make him more amenable to reason.

" 'You are most kind,' he replied in that same cultured dead voice. 'Thank you.' I hastened to drape the coat around his shoulders, and at my first touch, a miraculous transformation occurred. Life and intelligence returned to his countenance, and he stood and turned to face me.

" 'It has happened again,' he said to me, in a perfectly normal voice. 'I apologise for any trouble I have caused you. Ah!' He caught sight of the dead sparrow, and shuddered. 'This is what set me off. Anything like this can do it. Death or violence, or even some trivial incident that appears unconnected with such matters can make me weep without cause and become dead to the world.' He broke off and studied my face. 'Who are you and what are you doing here?'

" I introduced myself as a London friend of his father's who was staying at the Hall, omitting any mention of you (I assume that I acted correctly in this?) and adding the information that I was a doctor of medicine.

" 'You were brought here to attempt to cure me of... of this?' he asked.

" I answered, quite truthfully, that that was not the case, but that I was ready to lend whatever assistance I could if it were required, and he seemed to accept my explanation. As we talked, it came on to rain, falling lightly at first, but the downpour soon became quite heavy.

" 'I have your coat,' he said to me. 'Please allow me to return it to you.'

" I protested that I was wearing thick tweeds, which would absorb the water, and that his suit was made of lighter material which was less suitable for the weather, and accordingly we started back to the Hall, where we were met by the Earl, who expressed his gratitude to me for bringing back his son.

" He informed me that similar events had transpired in the past, and that it had proved extremely difficult, if not completely impossible, to persuade Hareby to return to the Hall on these occasions. He praised my efforts in no uncertain terms, and remarking the state of my saturated garments, ordered a hot bath to be prepared for me, and for Bouverie to take my wet clothes and restore them to a wearable state. I thanked him for his consideration, and went upstairs to my room.

" While I was making my way to my room, I encountered Lady Hareby, who seems bowed down with worry, the causes of which I need hardly spell out to you. In the course of our conversation, however, she made one or two observations to me which gave me distinct cause for concern regarding the future safety of her unfortunate husband. The implications that I inferred from our conversation seem to be that, imprimis, she wishes to be free of her marriage to him, and secundus, she would appear to be actively contemplating his death. Though I have no proof of this, she has given me ample cause for concern. She is also aware, though I have not informed her of the fact, that you and I are friends. I strongly suggest that you come up here as soon as convenient in order to avert the possible future tragedy that I sense is in the making."

Chapter IV

Lady Hareby

Y account above as presented to Sherlock Holmes, while accurate in most respects, nonetheless omits several important points, which I will now set down. In all honesty, I cannot omit them, though I am in no way proud of what occurred, or of my actions and feelings here, and subsequently throughout this case. However, if this account ever finds its way into the public gaze, I will most certainly ensure that none of what I am about to relate here makes its way into print.

After accepting Lord Darlington's offer of a bath and the care of my clothes, I retired to my room, and had stripped off most of my sodden garments, retaining only my undergarments, preparatory to donning my dressing-gown and taking my bath, which Bouverie had informed me was being prepared for me at the other end of the passage.

A knock came at the door, and I gave the command to enter. My back was turned, and I did not bother to face my visitor, supposing it to be Bouverie.

"You will find my clothes on the chair beside the bed," I remarked, still without turning.

"So I observe," came a female voice from behind me.

As one might imagine, I was considerably surprised, not to say shocked, by this. It is, after all, not the habit of the best houses to allow female servants to wait on male members of the family or guests, and I was astonished that Bouverie, who had so far impressed me with his bearing and competence, should allow such a state of affairs to prevail. I turned to face the speaker, and was astonished to see, not the servant that I had expected, but a young lady, in the full flush of her beauty, dressed in a green silk creation that appeared to my masculine eyes to be in the height of fashion. Tearing my gaze away from her oval face, framed in a mass of lustrous curled blond hair, I noticed that her condition was far advanced, in my professional opinion, at about the eighth month, I did not need to be my friend Sherlock Holmes to deduce that this was Lady Hareby, the wife of the poor unfortunate I had encountered earlier.

"Your Ladyship ... " I stammered, all too conscious of my dishabille.

"You would make me happier if you called me by my name, Elizabeth," she replied with a smile that had an almost physical effect on me. "I enquired of Bouverie who you might be, and discovered your name, so I am sure you will have no objection if I call you John?"

"Not at all," I replied, more than a little flustered by the circumstances under which I now found myself. "And what may I do for you ... Elizabeth?" I asked.

"I need to talk with you," she replied.

"Certainly. Please allow me to make myself more presentable, and I will be with you shortly."

"There is no need for that," she answered me, stepping inside the room and shutting the door behind her. She turned the key in the lock, removed it, and slipped it inside the bosom of her dress. Needless to say, I was more than a little taken aback by her boldness.

"Lady Hareby—" I began.

"Elizabeth," she corrected me.

"Elizabeth, then. This is hardly decent or proper. I insist that you leave my room at once and allow me to regain my decency."

"You insist?" She laughed. "A big brave soldier like you insisting on something from a weak helpless woman like me? And in my condition? Shame on you, you big bully." She advanced toward me, and tapped me playfully on the wrist.

To say that I was confused and embarrassed would be a severe understatement. "What if we are discovered together like this?"

"I assure you, John, that I will do nothing to give us away.

We only run the risk of discovery should you choose to inform the world, and I hardly think you will do that."

"At any rate, please return the key of the room to me," I insisted, more than a little discomfited by her use of my Christian name.

"When I am ready," was her answer, as she delicately patted the area of her anatomy where the key presumably currently reposed. My notice was naturally drawn to that part of her figure, which was truly of most pleasing proportions, and I found it hard to concentrate my attentions on the subject at hand.

"Very well, then. If you wish to talk now, please sit down." I busied myself clearing my clothes off the chair on which they were currently lying.

"I will sit on the bed," she answered, suiting the action to the words. "And you will sit beside me."

My confusion and embarrassment were now nearly at a peak. "I will sit where I please," I retorted.

"I think you will find it most pleasing to sit beside me," was her answer.

I said nothing, but remained standing.

"I see you are determined to please yourself," she mocked me, "rather than doing your duty as a host."

"My dear Eliz— Lady Hareby," I replied in as firm a tone as I was able to achieve under the circumstances. "With all due respect and deference, I am in a somewhat ambiguous position as a host. My guest is uninvited, and she has removed any possibility of her leaving without her consent to do so." I moved once more to the chair, and despite the fact that my garments were still wet, started to replace my clothing and cover myself decently. Before I could make much progress in this matter, I was interrupted by a sob from my visitor.

"So I am not welcome?" she replied. "You, too, spurn me?" Tears welled in her eyes as she looked at me with an expression of sadness on her face. Like any true man, I am powerless to resist a weeping woman, and I moved to sit by her side, temporarily heedless of my state of undress.

"Thank you," she said to me, withdrawing a lace handkerchief and dabbing it to her eyes. "I knew you would understand. Now, John," she continued, turning to face me, "I believe from what Bouverie told me that you have met my husband in one of his fits. What is your professional opinion?"

"I am a general doctor, rather than a specialist in such matters. Such diagnosis as I might provide is likely to differ from that of such a consultant. However, I have experienced such a case before in India, when one of my brother officers was struck on the head by a native whom he was attempting to restrain. The case was remarkably similar."

"And the result?" She leaned towards me and looked into my eyes. The scent of her perfume hung heavy in the air, providing me with yet another distraction.

"I ... I seem to remember that there was no cure."

As she opened her mouth to answer, there was a knock on the door, and Bouverie's voice could be heard.

"Excuse me, sir, but your bath is ready. I will take your clothes for cleaning and pressing while you are in the bathroom, if that is what you require."

I replied after a moment's thought. "Thank you, Bouverie. I am not quite ready. I fear I may have dozed off and have only just awakened. Another five or ten minutes should see me in the bath."

"Very good, sir." We could hear the sound of retreating footsteps.

"Very good, John," my visitor breathed. Her lips were close to my ear, and I could feel her warm breath. I stood up, but she clutched at my hand as I rose, and drew it to her breast.

"Do not go," she implored me. "Have you no pity?" I looked at her, questioningly. "Pity for a woman whose husband is a pitiful wreck of a man," she explained. "There is no hope for me as long as he lives, and there is no escape. Were he certified as insane, I could be free of him, but it does not seem that this well ever be the case. You have seen him for yourself, and you know that he can appear like any other man at times."

"So can many lunatics," I reasoned to her. "The fact that he may pass as healthy is no guarantee to a medical man that the balance of his mind may, indeed, be disturbed."

She clutched my hand tighter to her bosom, and I was now extremely uncomfortable at the close proximity to her in which I now found myself.

"So were he seemingly to die by his own hand, there would be no doubt at the inquest that he had indeed died as a result of killing himself?" she pressed me.

"Lady Hareby!" I snatched my hand away, one of the rings she was wearing scratching me slightly. "I cannot believe my ears! Have you the faintest notion of what you are saying? I warn you that were a coroner's jury to hear me repeat your words to them, things might go very hard with you."

"They would have to prove the meaning of what you have just implied by your words," she retorted coolly.

"I am not sure what you feel my words implied," I replied.

"Then a coroner's jury would probably have the same problem with my words, Doctor John Watson," she replied. "Do not accuse me of anything of which you are not certain. Surely your friend Mr. Sherlock Holmes would tell you that? I will leave you now. May I ask you," and here she glanced down significantly at her swollen belly, and extending a hand in my direction, "to assist me to rise. Do not worry, John, I am not about to steal your hand." I assisted her to her feet, and she reached inside her décolletage. "Let me out, please," she requested. "Please look and ensure that no-one is around to observe me leaving your room. That would never do, would it,

John? It might damage your reputation," she said, mocking-ly. I took the key, which retained the warmth from her body, and unlocked the door. A quick glance was sufficient to reas-sure me that my visitor could depart unobserved.

" Until later, then," she whispered to me as she slipped out. I was unsure as to her exact meaning, but I felt it boded ill for me.

I quickly wrapped my dressing-gown around me and made my way to the bathroom. Although the water was not hot as it had been, it still managed to revive my spirits somewhat and I was certainly in a more sanguine mood as I stepped from the tub and towelled myself.

Chapter V
The Cabinet
of the Mace

N returning to my bed-room, I discovered that the admirable Bouverie had removed my damp clothes and laid out a set of dry garments into which I changed, before penning the above report to Holmes.

By the time I had finished collecting my thoughts and putting them on paper, it was time for luncheon. The Earl and his daughter-in-law were waiting in the drawing-room as I entered.

" May I introduce my daughter-in-law, Elizabeth Hareby? " Lord Darlington said to me. " Elizabeth, this is Doctor John Watson, a friend from London, who will be staying with us for a few days."

" Enchanted," she replied, extending her hand, as if we had not met under somewhat more intimate circumstances an hour or so earlier. I was relieved to see that her dress appeared now to be of a somewhat more modest cut than that she had been wearing earlier, and put this down to the influence of the Earl.

" My father-in-law has been telling me what you did this morning for my husband," she said to me, " and I am most grateful to you for this. He still appears to be a little indisposed, and will not be joining us. Shall we go in to luncheon? "

The meal was a simple affair, and the conversation was chiefly between Lady Hareby and myself on the subject of London society. Though I myself am not a habitué of these circles, my natural interests, as well as my association with Sherlock Holmes, had given me some acquaintance with the persons to whom she referred, though I confess that many of the details to which she alluded were outside my sphere of knowledge.

After luncheon I sealed my report into an envelope, and handed it to Bouverie with instructions that it was to be delivered immediately. There seemed little advantage to my keeping Holmes' name a secret any longer, since it now appeared to be common knowledge, and I accordingly gave no instructions to Bouverie regarding his keeping the matter confidential.

In the afternoon, the Earl invited me to try my skill with the rod together with him in a small trout stream that ran near the copse in which I had discovered his son earlier. The rain that had soaked me earlier had now completely ceased, and I readily assented, for a number of reasons. In the first place, I had promised Holmes that I would provide companionship for the Earl, and his invitation to me was obviously made in all sincerity. Secondly, there was the chance that I would be able to discover more details regarding both the Earl's son and daughter-in-law. And finally, at that time of my life I was a keen fisherman, and the prospect of an afternoon's sport of this kind was a pleasant one.

Lord Darlington and I accordingly set out, suitably dressed and equipped. As we prepared ourselves for the coming battle of wits against the trout visible in the pools, he turned to me and spoke.

"Watson, you saw my son today. I realise that you have had little opportunity to study him or his behaviour, but do you have any opinions at this stage?"

I shook my head. "Few, I am afraid. My specialty is not in this area, so please do not take my word on the matter as final, but it seems to me that he would be better off in some kind of institution where he could receive care and treatment. This Hall is, after all, a rather isolated spot."

I received no immediate answer to my proposal, and the Earl continued to sort through his collection of flies in search of a suitably tempting morsel for the fish. Having attached his chosen lure to the end of the line, he spoke to me again.

"I shall bear your words in mind. The same thought has occurred to me, naturally, but I am reluctant to deliver him into the hands of others. What do you make of my daughter-in-law?"

" I fail to grasp your meaning, sir."

He snorted. " Come, man, I do not believe you are a fool. What do you think of her?"

" A young lady of considerable charm." I was unwilling to be drawn out further.

" She is a fortune-hunter, Watson, to put it bluntly. Her family had no money at all, and she married my boy Edgar simply for his money, of that I am convinced. She is indeed possessed of considerable charm, as you say, and it was that charm that she employed to trap my boy. Since his accident, she has pretended to care for him, but in my opinion she is the cause of much of his misery. She baits him, I am convinced, knowing his extreme tender-heartedness, which verges on weakness of mind, and she deliberately seeks out and places in his way those objects that will provoke him. Small dead animals, such as mice, and the like." The peer's normally placid face was flushed and angry as he related these things to me.

" To what end?" I could not help but ask.

" I can only assume that she seeks to tip the balance of his mind permanently, so that he will be declared insane, and thereby unable to inherit. The estate is, naturally, entailed in the male line, but the succession of the title as well as the estate is dependent upon the inheritor being " of sound mind and body" as the old document prescribes. If Edgar were to be declared insane, the succession would pass to his heir, his eldest son."

" And if there were no male heir?"

" Then the line would die out. I was an only child, as was my father before me. I have no close relations, and there is no-one to inherit. My opinion in this matter is that though the courts might possibly award the estate to my son's widow upon my death, I feel the possibility is remote. As for the title, since it cannot pass through the female line, it would become extinct, or possibly dormant. Now, let us fish and attempt to forget these matters."

He flicked his fly over a small pool and was almost instantly rewarded with a tug on the line. I helped him land the fish, which turned out to be a good one-pounder.

"A good start," I remarked, and I in my turn was rewarded by a similar catch after a few minutes. An hour's fishing brought one or two more fish each, the companionable silence between us being broken only by remarks relating to our angling activities.

At the end of this time, however, the Earl reverted to his previous topic of conversation. "I know that I can rely on your discretion here, so I am going to tell you that I am not sure, in any case, that the infant she is carrying is my grandson."

I looked at him. "You mean...?"

He nodded sadly. "Throughout the last season that she spent in London her conduct was notorious. Although well-meaning friends attempted to keep the news from me, stories of her escapades reached even my ears. I find it difficult to tolerate the woman in my house, Watson, though I must do so for the sake of my son." He looked up at the sky. "The clouds are moving in and it looks like rain. Let us return to the Hall. The fish will be a welcome treat at breakfast tomorrow."

The dinner that evening was a sombre affair. Lord Hareby joined us, but appeared to have withdrawn into himself, and the meal was eaten in almost total silence. Elizabeth Hareby sat at one end of the table, with Lord Darlington at the other, and though the food was ample, and well-cooked, it failed to satisfy.

After the meal, Lord Hareby listlessly expressed his intention of retiring, and his wife informed us that she would accompany him upstairs. The couple took their leave of Lord

Darlington and myself as we brought out the port, of which I alone partook, and cigars. After about twenty minutes of agreeable conversation on general matters, I asked to see the cabinet from which the jewellery and the Mace had disappeared. The Earl led me to the library, and pointed to a painting, drawing it to one side to reveal an iron cabinet in one corner of the room.

It was, however, the portrait that had covered the cabinet, now moved to one side, which arrested my attention. A rakish figure, clad in the height of the barbaric and opulent fashion of the days of Good Queen Bess, sneered down at us from his elevated position. The long face, framed in a dark beard, seemed to speak of the more unbridled passions of a former age, and cruelty, not unmixed with a certain generosity of spirit, was apparent in the countenance of the Tudor nobleman.

" That, I take it, is the third Earl ? " I enquired.

" The same. It was he who took Mad Maggie and held her captive, and he who first heard of the true meaning and power of the Mace." These words were spoken with the utmost gravity and sincerity, and it was clear to me that I was in the presence of a man who truly believed, no matter what protestations he might make, in the fantastical story of the legendary curse that had been laid upon his family.

I looked again at the portrait, and then at my host. Though at first sight there was little in the way of outward resemblance, my time with Holmes had taught me to examine often overlooked details, in particular, the shape of the ear, and I could distinguish a close resemblance between that of the subject of the portrait, where it had been particularly well delineated, and that of the present Earl.

" And the cabinet ? " I enquired, when I had gazed my fill of the portrait, whose mocking face seemed to be a presentiment of doom.

For answer, Lord Darlington withdrew the key, which as he

had said, was attached to his watch-chain, and applied himself to the lock. With a soft creaking sound, the door opened, revealing an iron box, fitted with shelves, and otherwise empty.

" Was the jewellery kept in cases? " I asked.

" No, it was wrapped in chamois leather to protect it from scratches, but there had never seemed to be any reason to keep it in boxes or cases. As I explained in London, it was not worn often, and was returned here as soon as the event occasioning its removal was over."

" And the Mace? "

" That was on the top shelf, by itself, and it reposed on a cushion of red velvet. The cushion also was removed by the thief, as you can tell."

I did not reply, but contented myself with examining the cabinet, which appeared to be of antique workmanship, with the fittings being of a somewhat primitive and rude construction, somewhat at odds with the modern Bramah lock. I remarked on this to the Earl.

" Yes, it does seem a little strange, perhaps, but the original lock, dating with the rest of the cabinet to the seventeenth century, had been unreliable for many years, and at last reached the point where it was unusable. The cabinet, as you can see, incorporates bars reaching into the mortar cementing together the stones of the walls, making it more trouble than it was worth to replace the cabinet in its entirety. I therefore arranged for the lock alone to be replaced." He closed the cabinet door, but due to the irregularity of the hinges, the door failed to close properly, and it was necessary for him to lift the door on its hinges and deal it a smart tap in order to ensure its safe closure. A loud metallic ring accompanied the door's falling into place. " That, Doctor, is the sound I heard on the night the Mace was stolen," remarked the Earl.

" I can readily understand how such a sound would awaken you," I replied.

We left the library, with its gallery of long-dead faces lining the walls, and Lord Darlington bade me a good night outside the room he was currently using as a bed-room, which as he had told Holmes and myself, was next to the library. With his hand on the heavy oak door, he said, with the utmost sincerity, " I cannot impress upon you strongly enough that it is vital that the Mace be recovered as soon as possible. My line, which has endured for centuries, will otherwise come to an end. Doctor Watson, these may seem like the ravings of an old man, but I urge you to regard my words as seriously as I do myself."

I could give no specific answer to this declaration, and had to content myself with wishing him a good night, and taking myself upstairs to my own bed-room.

Chapter VI

From the second report of John H. Watson to Sherlock Holmes

have discovered an interest I share with the Earl—that of fly-fishing. I know that you despise the occupation, but I have found that for me it provides a period of calm in my life during which I may reflect on various matters. It would appear it serves the same purpose in Lord Darlington's existence. While we were fishing he unburdened himself to me on the subject of the future disposition of the estate (entailed, as one might expect), in the event of his son's incapacity rendering him unfit to inherit. He also made his views clear on Lady Hareby, whom he described in less than flattering terms.

[Here I omit some clinical observations I made regarding the condition of Lord Hareby, which are of little interest other than to a fellow medical practitioner]

"... My conversation with the Earl while we were pursuing our angling has persuaded me that danger is in the air, and we may expect trouble from the quarter of Lady Hareby. As to her unfortunate husband, I am more and more convinced that his condition is not irreversible, and would respond to treatment were he to be removed to a suitable establishment. The foremost specialist in cases of this kind is Sir Giles Merryton, who is still teaching at Bart's, as I understand. In the event that you have the time to do so (unlikely, I agree), you may wish to consult him on the matter, quoting my earlier report, and the details I have given above. Maybe he could bring pressure to bear on the Earl regarding this subject, when the latter next visits Town.

"It is now eleven o'clock at night. I spent the latter part of the evening chatting pleasantly with Lord Darlington, regarding general matters, Lord and Lady Hareby having taken themselves to bed shortly after dinner.

"Lord Darlington and I also examined the cabinet from which the jewellery and Mace had been abstracted. In my view, the cabinet, though old and primitive in construction, appears secure enough, and it would be necessary for a key to be employed were it to be opened. Since the key is always close to Lord Darlington, and he assures me that it is the only one in existence, I am, quite frankly, at a loss to know how the items were removed from the cabinet.

"In public, despite Lord Darlington's report, and despite my earlier impressions, Lady Hareby seems a most attentive and dutiful wife in most respects, though I still entertain some serious doubts in this regard which I do not propose to put down on paper. I will now place this report in an envelope and give it to Bouverie first thing in the morning, and instruct him to send it to you post-haste.

"I should inform you that I am now certain of the identity of the thief who purloined the jewellery and the Mace from the cabinet. Please disregard my earlier request to consult Sir Giles, and come at once. I sense tragedy in the air, and pray to God that we will not be too late to prevent it."

Chapter VII
Lady Hareby & Dr. Watson

NCE again, the above text of my account for Sherlock Holmes was incomplete, and not within the strict bounds of truth. I had undergone another uncomfortable experience, of an intimate nature, which I saw no need to report to him in detail.

I had completed the report as above, other than the last paragraph, placed it in the drawer of my dressing-table, and changed into my night attire before locking the door to my room, shutting the window against the night air, and climbing into the luxurious canopied bed. It had been a long and demanding day, and I was soon in a dreamless sleep. The bed was comfortable, and the quiet of the surrounding countryside was a refreshing change after the ceaseless London bustle.

I was awakened in what I assumed to be the small hours of the morning by what I took to be a sound in my room, but it was hard for me to be certain of this, since rain had started to fall heavily, and the noise of the water tumbling down the roof into the gutters, and the rustle of the water on the leaves of ivy and other creeping plants that covered the walls of the Hall masked other sounds. I listened carefully, and heard what I took to be a board creaking as the wind dropped momentarily, and the noise of the rain ceased. I had just persuaded myself that this was my fancy, or at any rate, was a perfectly natural phenomenon, being unaccustomed as I was to the sounds peculiar to this old house at night, when the creaking sound was repeated, at regular intervals.

I sat up in bed, and fumbled for the box of matches that I knew was on the nightstand beside the bed in order to light the candle there, when I felt my arm gripped by a hand. Stifling the cry that rose unbidden to my lips, I cast about with my other hand, and discovered that the arm of the hand that had taken hold of me was bare of any clothing, and was soft and smooth. At that point, I knew the identity of my visitor, even before she spoke.

" Surprised to see me, John ? " she asked me in low tones. " Or rather, perhaps I should say, since you can see little in this light, surprised to feel me ? "

" Naturally," I stammered. " I am not accustomed to nocturnal visits of this type."

" I am not sure that I know, or indeed that you know what you mean," she replied. " I had assumed, though, that company at this hour under these circumstances might be somewhat unfamiliar to you. Now tell me, John, what did my husband's father have to say about you ? Did you write it all down in your report to Sherlock Holmes ? "

" How did you know I was writing reports to him ? " I asked, too surprised to deny it.

" Elementary, my dear John," she replied. " I noticed Bouverie taking a letter from you addressed to Mr. Sherlock Holmes earlier today. I am sure that my father-in-law unburdened himself to you while you were fishing together, and that you are bound in duty to make regular reports of all you see and hear to your friend. Is that not so ? "

" It may be so," I replied. " How did you gain entrance to my room ? " as the thought struck me. " I was under the impression that I had locked my door."

She laughed. " So you did," she replied. " A wise precaution, if there had only been one key in the whole of the house. Now, if you would," and the grip on my arm tightened, " I would like to read the report to your friend."

By now, I had recovered a little of my self-possession. " I have not yet started to write it. I had planned to prepare it first thing next morning, and hand it to Bouverie for posting before breakfast," I lied.

" And was I to feature in it ? " Her hand not gripping my arm made for my face, and I could feel her hand cupping my chin.

" It was to consist largely of a medical report on your

husband's condition that Holmes was to forward to a London specialist for his opinion."

"And nothing about me?" Her tone was almost petulant. "I am beginning to feel the cold, by the way. I think I would be more comfortable under the covers." Before I could do anything to stop her, she had lifted the covers of the bed, and was lying beside me. I attempted to move away, but found myself restrained by one of her arms around my neck. I was relieved to discover that she was wearing a long nightdress, albeit one with short sleeves that left her arms bare.

"Lady Hareby. Elizabeth," I protested. "Really, this is most—" I found myself at a loss for words. Once more, her warm breath tickled my cheek, and the scent of her filled my nostrils. "I must ask you to leave my bed and my room."

"Your bed? Your room?" she asked. "Remember, John, that you are a guest in this house. This house which will soon be mine, if all goes well. Then it will be my bed and my room, will it not?"

I had no answer to this, and I lay in silence, close to this beautiful but dangerous woman, exercising all my self-control to retain what I could of my composure.

"Poor little John," she mocked me. "I really had no idea you would be so moral about these matters. From the look of you, I had guessed you to be a dashing ladies' man. Obviously that is not the case."

I could feel myself blushing in the darkness. "Elizabeth, there is a time and a place for everything. I do not consider this to be the time nor the place for such a discussion."

Her response was a silvery laugh. "Dear me. If two in the morning is not a suitable time, and a bed is not a suitable place, when and where would be more suitable, my dear little doctor?"

"You know very well what I mean," I retorted angrily, breaking free as roughly as I dared, and springing out of bed. "You are welcome to spend the night in my bed, if that is what you choose to do, but I will not be in it." With as much dignity as I could manage, I groped for matches, lit my candle, gathered up my dressing-gown and retrieved the report I had written to Sherlock Holmes from the drawer where I had stored it. " I shall be spending the night in the drawing-room or some other location where I will not be disturbed. Sleep well." With that I closed the door firmly behind me.

CHAPTER VIII

DR. BRENDELL

AWOKE the next morning on the great sofa in the drawing-room. I had thrown over me a travelling-rug which I had discovered in the hall before I went to sleep, having first opened my report to Holmes, and added the lines I have reproduced above as the final paragraph. The dying fire in the grate had prevented the chill and damp of the night from pervading the room, and the warmth of the room, together with the comfort of the heavy rug, resulted in my sleeping well, despite the unfamiliarity of the surroundings.

Bouverie was drawing back the heavy curtains to admit the daylight, and as I stirred, he appeared to notice me for the first time, and started.

"Good Lord, Sir!" he exclaimed. "You gave me a bit of a turn there. Was your bed not comfortable, then, sir?"

I made some vague reply regarding the noise of the rain in the night on the roof outside my bed-room window, to which he merely replied, "Shall I have the hot water sent to your room, sir?"

I was reasonably certain that my nocturnal visitor would no doubt have returned to her own room, so I assented to that proposal, and made my way upstairs to dress and make my toilet. Before I could enter my room, though, I encountered one of the housemaids running down the corridor, shrieking like a steam-engine. I caught hold of her by the shoulders and gazed into her face.

"Whatever is the matter with you, woman?" I asked her. "Stop that noise and calm down."

"It's the master," she sobbed. "He's dead! Lying in his bed cold as ice!"

A thrill of horror went through my frame as she spoke these words. "Lord Darlington is dead?" I exclaimed, horrified.

"No, sir, it's not the old master. It's the young master, Master Edgar."

" I am a doctor. Let me collect my things, and then you can lead him to me." I hurried to my room, noting that my bed was unoccupied, and snatched up my doctor's bag. The housemaid led the way along the corridor to the room at the end and opened the door.

" He's in there, sir," she announced. " I must now go and tell the master what's happened." She left the room, stifling a sob as she did so.

I approached the bed's occupant, who lay like a waxen figure in the half-light from the partially drawn curtains, unmoving and seemingly lifeless. I pressed my fingers to his neck, feeling for a pulse, and to my surprise I discovered a weak fluttering heartbeat. A hand-mirror placed to his nostrils showed that he was breathing shallowly.

" What killed him, Doctor ? " came a voice from behind, startling me. I turned to see the Earl, who must have entered while my attention was engaged. He was gasping a little, clutching a stick in his hand, and I saw that he was in some pain, presumably from his gout. " What killed him ? " he repeated, almost collapsing into the chair beside the bed.

" I am happy to tell you, sir, that he is not dead."

" Thank God," said the old man fervently. " Thank God ! " he repeated.

" He is, however, in a very weak state, and I would strongly recommend that he is moved to the nearest hospital as soon as possible. If one of the servants can make the necessary arrangements to have a carriage prepared ? "

Lord Darlington gave the necessary instructions to Bouverie, who had entered the room.

" Wait," I commanded as the butler was about to leave. " Arrange for the carriage to be made ready. Make up some sort of bed within the carriage to allow the patient to be transported as comfortably as possible. While this is being done, dispatch one of the grooms or coachmen to the local doctor and ask him to come here. He will need to accompany the patient to the hospital. When that is done, a message should be sent to the hospital to inform the doctors there of what has occurred, and to allow them to make all necessary arrangements." I tore a leaf from my notebook, and scribbled a few lines to whomever might be in charge of such matters, folded it, and handed it to the butler. I paused before removing another leaf, wrote a few words on it, and handed it to him with a half-sovereign. " This telegram is to be sent to London as soon as you have arranged the other matters. It is reply-paid. Any money remaining after you have paid for it to be sent, you are to keep for yourself."

" Why, thank you, sir," he replied, departing.

" That telegram was addressed to Sherlock Holmes, of course, asking him to come here at once," I explained to the Earl. " Now let us look at my patient." I administered a few drops of digitalis to strengthen Hareby's heartbeat, and was soon rewarded by a faint stirring of his limbs and a slight flush of colour returning to his cheeks. " It is far too soon to say he is out of danger," I explained to his father. " However, the danger is by no means as great as it was when I entered the room."

" What could be the cause?" asked the Earl.

" It may be that he has suffered some sort of cardiac trouble—that is to say, the blood supply to the heart has been interrupted, causing it to cease beating. This may be due to a number of causes, and through it is typically associated with older people, the young and middle-aged are by no means immune."

" Could it be the result of ... " and here the old man paused, lowered his voice and looked about him, though we were by this time the only people in the room. " Could it be poison?" he continued.

" There are indeed poisons which could produce this effect,"

I answered in the same low tones. "And for that reason, I suggest that no-one except you or myself is allowed to enter this room, other than to remove your son to the hospital. However, please also bear in mind that this could be a perfectly natural event, with no human cause involved."

"You do mean no-one at all is to enter the room?" he asked me significantly. "You take my meaning, I am sure."

"Most certainly I do," I replied. "If she asks why she is not allowed in the room, it is by my orders as a doctor. She is to be informed that he is too weak to receive any visitors. In addition, I wish this room to remain as undisturbed as is possible under the circumstances before Sherlock Holmes arrives here. If there is any trace of foul play, he will discover it, believe me. Where does she sleep, by the way?"

For answer, he pointed to a door in the wall. "That door leads to a bathroom that is shared by Lord and Lady Hareby. On the other side of the bathroom is a similar door, leading to Lady Hareby's chamber," he explained. I rose and examined the door, noting that it had been bolted at top and bottom from inside the bed-room. The fanlight above the door appeared to be slightly ajar, but close to the ceiling as it was, it was impossible that anyone could have gained entry to the room through it, even if the gap had been substantially wider than three inches or thereabouts, its present width.

"I am thankful you are here, Doctor. If you had not been present, I do not know what might have been the outcome," added Lord Darlington as I returned from my inspection. He shook his head sadly.

"Let us not speculate on what might have been, tempting though it may be at times to indulge our fancies in that way," I told him. "I would like to dress and shave, if I might ask you to stay here while I do so," I said.

"By all means. By the way," eyeing me curiously, "how did you come to be roaming the corridors in that state of undress when you came across Sally, the housemaid?"

"That is a matter I would sooner not discuss at present, if you have no objection, sir. I believe, though, that I may be able to reveal this minor mystery at some point in the future."

"Very well. Off with you."

Years of campaign life had imparted to me the skills needed to wash hurriedly, shave and dress myself in a matter of minutes. I returned to the room where the Earl awaited me. "Now I feel that you must leave, sir. It will not be good for you to remain here, and there may be other members of your household who will need your presence. I would be grateful if you could arrange for my breakfast to be brought to me here, should the ambulance from the hospital not have arrived by the time the meal is served."

"Of course. It may be as well to take myself to visit my daughter-in-law, much as it pains me to do so," he replied, sighing. "Thank you for all your help and assistance in this matter, Doctor."

NCE he had gone, I took a closer look at my patient, for I was now forced to consider him as such. He was breathing was now considerably more regular, and his pulse, though still feeble, beat at fixed intervals. I judged that he was not in immediate danger, and cast about the room for any clues that might confirm my suspicion of possible foul play.

There was a tray containing medicine bottles, the labels of which I examined without touching them. The majority bore the inscription of a pharmacist in the nearest town, but the exception was a patent medicine often prescribed to stimulate liveliness and energy in cases of lethargy, one which I would not recommend for my own patients, but one which I believed to do no harm – something that could not be said of all such nostrums.

Other than this, there was nothing untoward in the room.

A decanter of water with a glass resting on it stood beside the bed, with the glass containing one or two drops of water, indicating that it had been used recently. On my applying my nostrils to the glass, I could smell nothing, implying that it had contained merely water. I made a note of all these facts in my notebook, remarking also that the curtains were only half-opened, and that the morning's hot water, now cooling, had been brought in by the housemaid and left on the dressing table.

There was a cough behind me, and I turned to see Mrs. Bouverie holding a tray. "May I put this down here, sir?" she asked me. "I'll just clear away these things," indicating the medicine bottles.

I dissuaded her from doing so, and accepted the tray holding my breakfast, balancing it on my knees while sitting in the armchair by the window.

"Will there be anything else, sir?" she asked me. "I trust that this meets your requirements?" referring to the porridge, eggs and toast.

"Indeed it does, thank you. The housemaid who discovered Lord Hareby. I believe Lord Darlington said her name was Sally ...?"

"That would be Sally Crowthorpe, sir."

"Could you please send her here? I would like to ask her a few questions. Please reassure her that she is under no kind of suspicion and that there is no blame attached to her. I merely require an account of her actions this morning while they are still fresh in her memory."

"Very good, sir." She bowed slightly and left. A few minutes later, the housemaid whom I had met in the corridor and who had informed me of Lord Hareby's condition, entered the room.

"Excuse me, sir, but I was told by Mrs. Bouverie just now that you wanted to speak to me?"

" Yes, that is correct. I would be grateful if you could tell me what happened this morning just before you discovered Lord Hareby here? "

" He's not dead, then? " I reassured her on that point, and she commenced her narrative. She had brought in the hot water for Lord Hareby to wash and shave, since he apparently preferred to perform his toilet in his own room, rather than the adjoining bathroom. She had noticed upon entering that the heavy curtains were half-drawn, giving her enough light to set down the jug and basin on the dressing-table. As usual, she had performed this action somewhat noisily, as this was Lord Hareby's preferred method of being awoken, " and he'd always liked us to do that, ever since he was a schoolboy," she assured me. However, contrary to his usual practice, he had not stirred, and failed to move even when she had deliberately made a loud noise intended to wake him.

On going over to the bed to examine him, she had seen him " white as them sheets he was lying on", as she put it, and apparently totally immobile and not breathing. Feeling him timidly, she had noticed that he was cold and did not respond to her touch. She had assuming him to be dead and run out of the door into the passage, frightened by what she had seen, where she had encountered me on my way to the bed-room.

" And you never touched anything, Sally? " I asked her. " Not the curtains, and not the medicine bottles? "

" No, sir, I never touched the curtains, and I'd never go near those bottles, sir."

" Did you ever know him to have the curtains open in the morning? "

She appeared to reflect on this. " No, sir. Not these past few years, at any rate. When he was a lad, maybe sometimes he'd wake up early and draw the curtains himself and sit there looking at the park outside. But he hasn't been doing that for some time."

" I see. Thank you, Sally."

She sketched a curtsey and left the room, leaving me to finish my breakfast.

I started to regret having imposed this lonely vigil on myself, but occupied my time by performing such duties of a physician as I was able. I was pleased to see that, although he showed no signs of regaining consciousness, the patient's condition appeared to remain stable and indeed, showed signs of improvement. I had not long to wait, though, before I could hear the sounds of a carriage drawing up below the window.

A few minutes later, two of the grooms, as I took them to be, knocked on the door. The older of them I recognised as Hanshaw, who had met and transported Lord Darlington and myself from Berwick station. They had assembled some kind of stretcher on which to carry the patient, and though somewhat crude, I pronounced it perfectly fit for the purpose. " Let us wait for the doctor to arrive, as I believe he should be travelling to the hospital with his Lordship," I told them. A thought struck me.

" Was either of you men with Lord Hareby when he had his accident some months ago that was the cause of his trouble ? " I asked them.

Hanshaw answered for both of them. " No sir, though we were all out that day with the hunt. We were whippers-in that day, and we were with the hounds but of course his Lordship was riding. From what I heard, his horse stumbled over a rabbit-hole and fell, and he was thrown off and hit his head on a stone. Knocked out cold, he was. Jim here and me brought him back on a hurdle, but he was in a real sorry state. His head had been split open, and he was all over blood," he added with what seemed to be a certain relish. " Begging your pardon, sir, but can I ask what's up with him now ? "

" I suppose there is no harm in your knowing something of the matter. I suspect it to be connected with his heart," I answered.

"Ah, his heart. He's got a good heart, has the young master. Or he had one, anyway, until the accident. Not like some," replied the one who had been referred to as "Jim". "After the accident, he changed, as I suppose you've been told, sir."

I had no immediate answer to give to that, and was relieved to see Bouverie returning, with an elderly man in a black frock-coat, gripping a black bag, whom I took to be the local doctor.

"Brendell," he introduced himself, holding out a hand for me to shake. "Glad you were here, Dr.—"

"Watson. John Watson," I introduced myself. "Are you Lord Hareby's usual physician?"

"When he is at the Hall, yes."

"Have you observed a previous weakness in his heart?"

"Yes, indeed. He suffered from rheumatic fever as a young boy, and it left him with a permanently strained heart. Has he suffered from some kind of strain on the heart?"

"That is my belief," I answered. "I administered a few grains of digitalis, which seem to have afforded some relief. A word in your ear, Doctor Brendell, if you please?"

We moved away from the two grooms, and I asked him about the large number of medicine bottles by the side of the bed.

He gave me a smile which I could only interpret as being conspiratorial. "Most of them are nothing but water or alcohol," he confided in a whisper. "The old Earl is adamant that something be done for his son in this condition, and quite frankly, this case is beyond my comprehension. I believe that the placebo effect of these bottles does no harm to the patient, and increases the confidence of those around him, if you take my meaning. I assure you there is nothing there that can do him any harm."

I was somewhat revolted at this cynical attitude towards my profession, but endeavoured to hide my feelings. However, I felt it incumbent upon me to say something. "If you felt the case was outside your sphere of competence, surely it was your duty to ensure that he received treatment at the hands of those better able to supply that care," I remarked.

"That's as may be, Doctor," he replied, "but I have a living to make."

At this point, I was having severe doubts as to the wisdom of allowing Lord Hareby to travel to the hospital in the company of this doctor, whose competence I had no means of knowing, but whose attitude towards his patient gave me cause for worry. I was torn between my duty to Holmes and to justice, which demanded that I stay in the Hall, ensuring that no evidence of any possible criminal activity was disturbed or destroyed, and my duty to my Oath, which bound me to take care of my patient.

However, Brendell seemed to sense my dilemma. "Doctor Watson," he addressed me. "I may be an old man, and my medical technique may not be as advanced or as up-to-date as yours, but I do care for my patients. Believe me, Lord Hareby will be well attended in his journey to the hospital."

This reassured me somewhat, and I supervised the transfer of the unconscious man, following the stretcher down the stairs to the carriage drawn up outside the front door of the Hall, which had been admirably equipped for his transfer to the hospital. I saw him safely into the carriage, which trotted away down the drive, and as I turned back to re-enter the Hall, I saw Bouverie, mounted somewhat incongruously on a bicycle, coming the other way towards me. I waited until he arrived at the steps leading up to the front door and dismounted.

"The telegram has gone off to London, sir," he informed me. "If there is a reply, I have arranged for it to be brought here as soon and as quickly as possible."

"Excellent," I replied, and entered the Hall, and mounted the staircase. When I returned to the room, I discovered Lady

Hareby standing beside the now empty bed. I inwardly cursed my folly in leaving the room, but recollected that the justification I had previously given regarding the prohibition on entering the room, that the patient should not be disturbed, no longer held good, and that there were few satisfactory reasons I could give for continuing the ban on her entry.

O, Doctor," she greeted me, " I suppose we have reason to be thankful that you are with us today? According to my father-in-law, your diagnosis is that my husband has suffered some sort of disorder of the heart."

" I believe that to be the case."

"And what, in your professional opinion, would be the cause of this?" She stood, framed against the light from the window, which shone through her hair, creating an aureole of gold around her face, and making it difficult for me to judge her expression.

" There are many ways for such a condition to occur," I told her. " It can be the result of strain and stress, either physical, mental or emotional. It can occur in patients who seem otherwise seem healthy. To be frank, modern science is still at somewhat of a loss when determining the cause of such things."

" Could it be caused by artificial means? Would it be possible for another to induce such a condition?"

" It is possible, but impossible to determine with any certitude at this stage." I was unwilling to commit myself to any definite statements when talking to this woman, whom I could not help but suspect of some nefarious activities.

" And you have sent him to the hospital together with Dr. Brendell?" she laughed. " That old charlatan."

" What reason have you to call him by that name? " I asked her.

" Doctor John Watson, I had assumed that your association with Sherlock Holmes had led you to observe things that escaped ordinary mortals. Obviously that is not the case. Dr. Brendell learned his medicine in another age, as is made painfully apparent every time I go to Town to consult my physician in Harley Street."

" If you have such a low opinion of him, why do you allow him to continue treating your husband? "

She gave a bitter laugh. " Some decisions are not mine to make," she replied. " He has been the family's doctor for many years now, and it would take an earthquake to shake my father-in-law's opinion of him. But you are assuming, are you not, Doctor, that I truly wish to make a change in the treatment of my husband? "

I had no answer to this, since her words coupled with her physical proximity as she took a step towards me, baffled me and left me unable to arrange my thoughts, not for the first time since I had arrived at Hareby.

" Never mind," she said mockingly, observing my perplexity. " I can see that I will learn nothing from you. Maybe there is nothing in you to be learned, anyway." She held her head high, and with an audible sniff, swept out of the room.

Looking at my watch, I guessed that several hours would elapse before Holmes arrived, and I resigned myself to a lengthy wait. I glanced at the few books in the room, both to determine if there were some suitable reading material that would enable me to pass the time, and as a way of discovering, if possible, some more about the character of the unfortunate invalid. Not altogether to my surprise, I discovered that all the books concerned themselves with ghosts and superstitions, and all appeared to have been purchased from London booksellers in the past few months ; that is to say, following the unfortunate hunting accident.

I took down one of these books as a way of passing the time, and soon found myself engrossed, despite my better judgement, in a book telling of a house which, if the story were to be believed, had more spirits of the departed than of the living inhabiting it. The story was presented as one of sober fact, and I could not help but smile as I read the tales, imagining how Sherlock Holmes would disperse these superstitious fancies with his incisive reasoning powers. I had finished the first chapter, which continued to make me chuckle, even though that was almost certainly not the intention of the author, and found myself drawn to read the rest, much against my usual habit.

The book took quite some time for me to finish, and somewhat to my surprise, I found myself reaching for the next book on the shelf after that, having found the first volume to be at the least an entertaining way of whiling away the hours. I was interrupted by the butler, Bouverie, who brought me the telegram from Holmes informing me that he was coming to Hareby, and who also, to my surprise, informed me that it was time for lunch. I felt it was not advisable for me to move away from my post, and I requested that a tray be once more brought to me. I informed Bouverie of the train that would be bringing Sherlock Holmes, and asked that a carriage be sent to meet him at Berwick station.

The lunch was excellent, and it was hard for me to keep my eyes open when I had finished it, but the book I was reading held sufficient interest to keep me from falling asleep completely, though the volume slipping from my hands once or twice brought me to full consciousness with a jerk.

Chapter IX

Mr. Sherlock Holmes

T length, the sound of wheels outside the window told me that a carriage had arrived, and my guess that it was the carriage that had transported Sherlock Holmes from the station was confirmed when my friend entered the room some minutes later. He was dressed in clothes suitable for the country, in a suit of tweed, and a heavy ulster, with his flapped travelling-cap on his head.

" Well, Watson, I caught some of the news of the excitement from my worthy coachman. Lord Hareby was taken ill this morning, it appears, and is now in hospital at your orders. What is your diagnosis ? "

" Heart," I replied, " though I am unsure as to whether it is a natural strain on the heart or has been induced by some person or persons unknown."

" You suspect foul play, then ? "

" It would be easier to give you this than for me to explain," I answered him, handing him my second report which had remained unsent in my pocket for the whole day.

He scanned it through briefly. " Why did you write this in two different places, and what caused your agitation ? "

" How did you ... ? "

" Tush, man, it is simple enough. The quality of the ink and the shape of the pen nib both change halfway through the document, showing that you were in a different location using different implements. If that were not enough, note how the first part of the note blotted on the opposite side when the paper was folded, but not the addendum. Why? Because the addendum was written long after the first part, and the ink was allowed to dry, whereas it was not for the first part. As to the agitation of spirit, it is obvious in the way you form the loops of the 'y 's and the upstrokes of the 'l 's and 'h 's. The pen also digs deeper, almost tearing the paper in places. One would quite believe you had seen a ghost."

I could feel myself flushing, but felt the time was

inopportune to tell Holmes of the nocturnal visit of Lady Hareby to my bed-room. With a rare tact, Holmes refrained from questioning me further on the matter, though it must have been more than obvious to him that something was amiss in my manner.

He made his way to the bedside table. "With your medical background, what do you make of this?" he asked me, indicating the mass of bottles and potions. "What do they indicate to you?"

"That there are rogues in the medical profession, sad to say. I was told by Doctor Brendell, who has charge of the case of Lord Hareby, that the majority of the prescribed medicines are little more than placebos—that is to say, harmless mixtures which have no effect on the taker. His reason for this is to maintain his position as the family doctor. He is baffled by the case, and has no wish to admit it to Lord Darlington for fear of losing a lucrative case, so has adopted this method of 'treating' his patient."

"At least he does no active harm in this way," commented Holmes, with more than a touch of cynicism in his voice. "So all these are merely water or some such?"

"Other than the patent medicine in the bottle with the orange label. That contains a little alcohol, caffeine and some extract of the coca plant, as a general restorative."

"Which one is that?" asked my friend. "I see no such bottle here."

"It is the one just— " I checked my words, as I failed to discern the bottle in the place where I had first seen and remarked it. "Holmes, it is gone! "

"You are sure it was there?" he asked, somewhat dubiously.

"How can you doubt my word?" I pulled out my notebook in which I had sketched the disposition of the bottles as I had observed them.

"Very good, Watson," he remarked after a minute's study.

"You have demonstrated a truly excellent attention to detail. Now we must ask ourselves who could have taken it, when they did this, and why they did so. Have you been in the room all the time?"

"I confess that I went out of the room for a few moments when Lord Hareby was transferred to the carriage to take him to the hospital. Maybe an unpardonable lapse, but I felt in that particular instance that my duty was to the sick man."

"I cannot blame you," said Holmes. "Though I am unlikely to encounter the horns of exactly the same dilemma, I would almost certainly have done the same as you under the circumstances. Have you any suspicions that anyone might have entered the room while you were away?"

"More than a suspicion, I fear," I told him. "When I returned after seeing Hareby into the carriage, his wife was in the room."

"I see. And obviously you suspect her, though I see you have some reasons for not telling me the whole story. Never mind, my dear Watson, we will cross that bridge when we come to it. I perceive, though, that this is not the time to do so."

I guessed that Holmes had deduced my state of mind from my agitation, and therefore refrained from asking him about the processes that had led up to that statement.

"So you suspect foul play?" he asked me. "Are there any other facts you have observed that would support that idea?"

"When I entered the room this morning, the curtains were drawn halfway back. I spoke to the maid, and she informed me that they were in that state when she first entered the room."

"That is an interesting piece of data," replied Holmes. "Last night was a new moon, and there would be no light from outside at night. We must therefore conclude that the curtains were drawn back this morning after sunrise, if they were drawn back for the purpose of admitting light to the room. This window faces north-east, does it not, judging by the current position of the sun? We can therefore conclude that if the curtains were drawn for the purpose we have just described, it would be in the early morning."

" What other purpose can you imagine? " I asked.

" Why, for the purpose of entry, naturally," he answered. " As I was driving, I noticed that the outside walls of the Hall are covered with some creeping plant that would provide excellent assistance to any person attempting to climb up to the window. I take it you have not checked for signs of entry? "

" The thought never occurred to me," I confessed.

" Well, then," said Holmes, withdrawing a large magnifying lens from his pocket, and moving to the window. He used the lens to examine the catch and the wide window-sill thoroughly, before dropping to his knees and subjecting the carpet under the window to the same intense scrutiny. " No," he declared at length, " no-one appears to have entered through the window. Let us make perfectly sure." He grasped the catch and forced the casement window, which made a loud creaking sound as he pushed it open. " That sound alone is enough to tell us that there has been no attempt to gain entry through this route," he said. " Furthermore, if we examine the ivy outside, there is no disturbance to the leaves or twigs such as we would expect from such an attempt. Assuming, as we may, the curtains to have been drawn in the early morning, this would have been done for the purpose of admitting light. These curtains are remarkably thick, and I can imagine that if they were closed," twitching the curtains shut, " as you can see, it would be almost impossible to carry out any kind of action in this room."

" What sort of action? " I asked.

" That, Watson, is what we are to find out. In your experience as a medical practitioner, I ask you once more whether you consider that Lord Hareby's heart trouble to be natural or caused by some malicious influence?"

"It is quite frankly impossible for me to answer that question."

"Let me put a slightly different question to you? Would it be possible to produce a feeling of fear or terror in Lord Hareby such that it would result in the illness you have diagnosed?"

"In the usual run of things, I would say that it was not possible for an ordinary healthy man to suffer in that way. However, as you know, Lord Hareby was by no means healthy, and his nerves had been shattered as a result of his accident. I would say it was perfectly possible for that to have taken place. But I have no idea what sort of horrors you are suggesting, Holmes."

Nor I," he shrugged, "at present. Let us admit light to the chamber once again," reaching up to the curtain. "Halloa!" he cried, staying his hand. "Do you see something?" pointing to a spot on the carpet at the foot of the bed that appeared to be glowing with a pale green fire.

"I see it, but it is a trick of the light, surely?"

"Not so. May I trouble you to go to that spot and put your finger by it. Take care not to cover it or touch it."

I did so, and perceived that the spot indeed appeared to be glowing with its own light, rather than being a reflection or some such, as I had first suspected. Holmes drew back the curtains, and the spot faded.

"Aha!" Holmes exclaimed as he joined me, and brought his lens to bear on the portion of the carpet beside my finger. "I believe we have a spot of phosphorus here. Most unusual. Watson, mark down the exact position of this spot." He drew a folding rule from his inside pocket and measured the distance from the bed and from the walls, calling out the readings, which I then duly noted in my notebook. He then stooped down once again, and carefully used the point of his penknife to pick up the almost invisible speck of material and transfer it to an envelope.

"What is the meaning of this, Holmes?" I could not help asking him.

"If I knew, I would be a happy man. Stay, what is this?" He picked up a length of white thread, about six inches in length.

"A piece of thread which once held a button to a garment which has been torn off."

Holmes was once again employing his lens, and he shook his head. "No, that is not the case," he said. "If it had been employed in the manner you suggest, we would see some signs of folding, and wear on the outer surface of the thread. As it is, it is perfectly obvious that this has never been used in that fashion. Observe the small fibres protruding at right angles to the direction of the thread. They would not be present were the thread have been used in a garment. But why, Watson, why?"

He cast around the room, and suddenly turned to me. "Were you sitting in that chair there while you were reading?"

"Why, yes."

"And you moved the chair, I see?"

"I may have turned it slightly to catch the light, yes."

"But it was not here?" Holmes gestured to a spot near to where the glowing speck of phosphorus had lain.

"Not at all," I answered. "What makes you assume that it should ever have been there?"

"The indentations on the carpet clearly indicate that the chair has been positioned here in the recent past. Maybe the carpet is not ideal as regards showing the footprints of those who have walked upon it, but for a heavy item of furniture, such as that armchair, it retains the impressions admirably. See, are these not obvious to you?" He pointed at a small square depression, almost invisible, in the carpet, which was

echoed by three others, the four forming a square correspond-
ing to the legs of the armchair in which I had been sitting.

"Now that you point them out, I can see them, but without
your aid, I freely admit that I would never have seen them."

"How many times must I impress the point upon you,
Watson, that you see but you do not observe? But no matter."
He stood with his hands plunged deep in his trouser pockets, gazing at the floor, seemingly lost in thought. Suddenly
his head jerked upwards, and he remained motionless, staring
at the ceiling, again rapt in some inner deliberations. After
a full minute, he abruptly appeared to pull himself together,
and addressed himself to me.

"I think I have seen all that is required here at present," he
said to me. "Come, show me the cabinet from which the jewels and this Mace have been abstracted."

LED the way downstairs to the library, and as we
were about to enter it, Holmes stopped me. "Do
you know which room Lord Darlington is using as
his bed-room?" he asked.

"That one there," I replied, pointing to the oaken door next
to the one we were about to enter. Holmes merely nodded,
and we entered the library.

Holmes appeared to notice the portrait that had caught my
attention the previous evening when I had entered the room
in company with Lord Darlington, but he proceeded immediately with moving it to one side, before beginning an examination of the cabinet, initially concentrating on the lock.

"Yes, as we were told," he remarked. "A Bramah lock. I
think we can rule out any possibility of its being picked. As
you are aware, such a lock can be picked only with extreme
difficulty, and then only by an expert in these matters. Even
for me, the opening of such a lock can take as long as fifteen

minutes." He then moved to an examination of the cabinet itself. " The hinges would appear to be somewhat frail, relative to the cabinet itself. Let us see." His overcoat pockets proved to contain a small tool-kit, stored in a canvas roll. Taking out a metal spike and a hammer, he gently tapped out the hinge-pins of the cabinet.

" I had believed," he said to me, " that it would be possible to remove the door easily once the pins of the hinges had been removed in this way, but it appears there is some sort of internal lip or flange preventing this." He replaced the pins. " Did Lord Darlington inform you of the method by which this is secured to the wall ? "

" I saw for myself when it was opened that the bars of the frame are let into the masonry of the walls."

Holmes tugged at the cabinet, but failed to move it. " We must therefore assume that it was opened with a key," he said. " We have been informed of the existence of one key only, on the Earl's watch-chain. Therefore—" He broke off his discourse, and pointed at the wooden panelling that covered the walls. " Watson, do you see ? " His voice was hoarse with excitement.

" I think I do," I replied. " There is now a slight gap in the panelling. Your assault on the cabinet appears to have loosened one of the wooden panels."

" I wonder...? " he remarked, half to himself. His ever-ready pocket knife came into play once more, this time inserted between the wooden panels, and he used it gently as a lever. Without warning, the panel next to the cabinet came away, revealing a cavity, into which Holmes plunged his hand. " I can feel the side of the cabinet," he reported. " And there appears to be some sort of grip or handle here. Ah." He made some sort of effort, and withdrew his hand from the cavity in the wall, a metal sheet in his grasp. " This, Watson, is the side of the cabinet. I can now," placing his hand once more into the cavity, " extract from or place into the cabinet whatever I please."

" Wonderful ! " I exclaimed. " You have solved the mystery of how the jewels and the Mace were removed."

" Other than the fact that Lord Darlington informed us that he heard the sound of the door closing," he reminded me.

" I had forgotten that."

" Can you remember the sound you heard last night when the cabinet door was closed ? "

" I believe I can do that."

" Was it similar to this sound ? " he asked, replacing the metal sheet, with some obvious effort, as a metallic clang filled the room.

" Not unlike, certainly."

" And let us remember that there are two thick oak doors between here and Lord Darlington's bed, and also that Lord Darlington, by his own admission, is somewhat hard of hearing. A man wakened from sleep is unlikely to have a clear recollection of the sound that woke him. I think, Watson, we have now solved the mystery of how the jewels were taken. We still do not know why they were abstracted, or by whom. Truly a house of mysteries, eh ? " He replaced the wooden panel, covering the cavity in the wall, and stepped back. " He's a beauty, isn't he ? " he said, referring to the portrait of Earl Edward now hanging once more above the cabinet. " There is something to be said for those old days, do you not think ? "

" Certainly not," I replied, indignantly. " How can you say such a thing? The blessings of modern civilisation make for a much more peaceful and harmonious life."

" I must confess I was not altogether serious in making that judgement," he replied. " Still, there is something to be said for the simplicity of the past ages. Come, though, I hear voices outside, at least one of which I take to be that of our host."

We left the library, and as Holmes had surmised, the Earl

was standing in the entrance hall, talking to Bouverie, and presumably giving him orders. He broke off as we approached.

" Ah, Mr. Holmes," he exclaimed. " I am delighted to see you, even though the occasion is a sad one."

" So Dr. Watson has been informing me," replied my friend.

" And I see that he has been showing you the library ? "

" Indeed he has."

" Do you have any idea as to who might have abstracted the contents of the cabinet ? "

" It is impossible for me to say at present," replied Holmes.

" I understand. You have only just arrived here, naturally. Bouverie has shown you to your room ? "

" He has indeed, thank you."

" Will you take tea now ? "

Holmes accepted the invitation with alacrity.

" Good, good," replied the Earl. " This way, Mr. Holmes, please," as he led the way to the drawing-room, where Lady Hareby awaited us, seated behind a table on which stood a steaming teapot and plates of assorted dainties.

Holmes bowed slightly to her as he took her hand and introduced himself.

" Ah, the celebrated Sherlock Holmes," she murmured. " I do hope that you will entertain us with stories of your exploits while you are here."

" I am afraid that my talents do not extend in that direction," replied Holmes. " Should you require entertainment, you must look to my friend and colleague, Dr. Watson here."

" Ah, I fear that Dr. Watson provides poor entertainment," she replied, with a half-smile in my direction, which did not escape Holmes' keen eye.

" Is that so ? " he answered, releasing her hand, which he had retained in his own grasp throughout this exchange, for a somewhat longer time than etiquette would seem to permit. " Then you must work harder to persuade him."

There was an undercurrent to this conversation that, as you may well imagine, was disturbing to me, and I rapidly attempted to divert the flow by requesting a cup of tea from our hostess. This tactic appeared to have had the desired effect, as the topic now turned to the everyday business of tea and refreshments.

At one point the conversation turned to pet cats, and Holmes enquired of Lady Hareby if any of these animals were kept as pets at the Hall.

"No," she replied. "We used to have some at the stables, but I never went near them. I find them to be dirty and flea-ridden." She shuddered delicately. "And we do not keep any in the Hall. My father-in-law's retrievers would feel jealous, I fear."

While we were partaking of the tea and cakes, I noticed that Holmes appeared to be in a state of suppressed excitement, perhaps discernible only to myself as a result of my association with him. When we had finished the repast, Holmes stretched himself and yawned, apologising as he did so.

"I am sorry," he said to the company at large. "I slept very badly last night, and the journey up here was a little fatiguing. If I may, I would like to go upstairs and rest a little?"

"By all means, my dear fellow," replied Lord Darlington. "Do you have everything you need in your room?"

"I am certain that I have everything I require, other than a book Watson has in his room that I lent to him before he came here from London, and to which I would now like to refer. Watson, would you please come upstairs with me and let me have that volume?" This last was delivered looking at me, and accompanied by a surreptitious wink that reassured me that Holmes was, for purposes as yet unknown to me, being less than open about matters.

S soon as was polite, Holmes and I thanked our hostess, and made our way upstairs.

"Let us talk in your room," said Holmes. His eyes fairly burned with excitement. Once inside my room, he turned to me. "I have found the Mace!" he exclaimed.

"Where is it?"

"It may be a good idea to leave it where it is for now," he replied, somewhat vaguely. "That depends partly on the answers to the questions I am about to put to you. Firstly, did it rain last night? I assume it did, given the state of the fields on the way from the station, but I wish to be certain, and would also like to know what time the rain fell."

"It did indeed rain last night. I am unsure as to what time it stopped, but it started at about one or two o'clock, I would say." I had a recollection, though I had not actually remarked the hour myself, of Lady Hareby mentioning the time of night at some point in our nocturnal conversation.

"Did the noise disturb you?"

"I believe it woke me, yes. The lead roof of this building certainly resonates when water falls on it and the noise of the water dripping on the leaves of the creeper covering the walls is disturbing."

"Hmm ... " Holmes sauntered over to my bed. "Watson?" His tone was sharp. "I fear you are withholding something from me. How can you expect me to take on a case of this type if I am provided with only part of the information I need?"

"What are you talking about?" I was aware that my voice probably betrayed my anxiety, but I had no wish to confess the events of the past day and night to Holmes.

He shook his head. "I see a curled blonde hair on the pillow here, Watson. The only person I have observed here with such hair is Lady Hareby." He paused, and regarded me with a look that was more questioning than censorious.

I sighed. " As always, Holmes, you are correct in your deductions. However, though you are correct in inferring that Lady Hareby occupied this bed for part of last night, any other inferences you may have drawn are almost certainly mistaken." Despite myself, my voice had grown louder, and even to my ears sounded a little shrill.

A look of concern came over Holmes' face. " My dear fellow," he exclaimed. " Though I may sometimes chaff you a little over your partiality with regard to the fair sex, I trust that I know you well enough not to accuse you of immorality."

" Thank you," I replied, a little mollified by his words. I proceeded to give him an account of my dealings with Lady Hareby, during which he said little. At the end, he stood a while in silence, thinking.

" I really do not see that you have any reason to reproach yourself," he said to me. " It is hard to know how you could have done any other than what you did under the circumstances. And what you have told me also gives me pause for thought. It was raining, you say, when you became aware that she had entered the room ? "

" That is so."

" And was it the noise of her entry that woke you, do you think ? "

" Upon reflection, it may well have been, though I had ascribed my waking to the noise of the rain on the roof, I suppose that the noise of her opening the door could have been the cause."

" And she was in possession of a key to your room ? "

" On both occasions, yes."

" Which presumably means that she has keys to every room in the house, would you not say ? "

" I would assume so."

" In any case, it would seem advisable to wedge a chair under your door-handle tonight to prevent any more unwanted nocturnal invasion. It seemed to me on my observing her just now that she has, shall we say, set her cap at you, for whatever reason, and quite apart from any feelings of morality you may entertain on the subject, I feel it would be extremely inadvisable to accede to any wishes she may have in this matter." He clapped me on the shoulder. "Cheer up, man. You have nothing for which you need blame yourself in any way, embarrassing as the situation has been for you so far, and indeed, will continue to be so. I happen to know that you are not the first man to have been placed in such a position, even with Lady Hareby."

"Indeed? Lord Darlington intimated as much yesterday while we were fishing."

"Yes, my researches in London yesterday were most illuminating. I discovered that Lady Hareby has acquired a somewhat unenviable reputation, especially since her husband's accident. At least one other member of the nobility, two Members of the House of Commons, and a Queen's Counsel were mentioned to me in connection with her name, as well as a prominent Harley-street specialist. I do not consider that any kind of liaison with this woman would be to the advantage of any reputation other than her own. She does, indeed, appear to have acquired a kind of dark glamour surrounding her name."

I confess that in many ways I felt relieved. It appeared that I could perhaps regard myself as being, in one particular regard at least, as being the superior of those whom Holmes had just listed.

"Thank you for those words," I told him. "They have put my mind a little at ease."

"And now," replied Holmes, "for the Mace."

"You know where it is?"

He nodded. "Follow me," he said, leading the way out of my room to that formerly occupied by Lord Hareby.

"I looked carefully around that room. I saw nothing," I objected.

"You observed nothing," Holmes reminded me again. "You saw everything, I am sure, but you failed to make the necessary connections."

"Those being?" It was actually a relief for me to be engaging with Holmes in this kind of sparring, as opposed to his questioning me about personal matters.

"Remember, Watson. How were the curtains when you entered the room? Like this?" adjusting them as he spoke.

"Yes, indeed."

"And we agreed, did we not, that no-one could have entered through the window?"

"We did."

"What, however, if the purpose of opening the curtains was the opposite of entry?"

"You deduced, though, did you not, that no-one had used the creeper to assist with climbing up the wall? Would you not say that the same is true of an attempt to climb down the creeper?"

"I never claimed that a person had climbed down," he replied. "Simply that it was a method of exit."

"If not the exit of a person, then of what?" I asked, incredulously.

For answer, he forced open the window, and thrust one arm through the opening, a look of concentration on his face. "Aha! We have it!" he fairly shouted in triumph, bringing his arm inside once more. In his hand, delicately gripped at one end between his forefinger and thumb, was a twisted stick-like object, about two feet long. At the other end to that which Holmes was holding, a blackened disk seemed to be affixed, or rather, had been driven in.

"The Mace!" I exclaimed.

"I believe so," he replied. "See here," pointing to the end

in which the disk resided. " Here are the slits in which the previous coins have resided."

" So I see," I remarked. " It appears to be coated with some kind of substance. From the creeper covering the wall, do you think ? "

Holmes shook his head and smiled. " No, Watson. Let us conduct a little experiment. Let me stand here, and you close the curtains to shut out the light. I did so, and could not restrain my cry of astonishment.

" It shines in the dark, Holmes ! " Sure enough, the Mace, held in Holmes' hands, appeared to float in mid-air glowing with a faint green light, which faintly illuminated his face.

" As I suspected," he replied. " Open the curtains." I did so, and the glow faded from the Mace. " Now," continued Holmes. " You met and conversed with Lord Hareby, did you not ? In your opinion, if he were to be awoken in the dead of night, and were to see this in mid-air at the end of his bed, what would be the result ? "

" I am merely a general practitioner," I replied.

" Even so," Holmes pressed me, " your opinion is worth more than that of a layman in these matters."

" If I were pressed, I would have to conclude that the shock could cause one of two things. Firstly, it could send him into that depressed and febrile state in which I encountered him yesterday. It could also produce a physical effect in addition or instead of that mental shock. That physical effect would take the form of a severe strain on the heart, as we observed." I stopped as the full implications of what I was saying became apparent to me. " What you are implying is that this Mace was introduced specifically in order to incapacitate poor Lord Hareby ? "

" That is exactly my deduction."

" Someone entered the room at night and brandished this, in an attempt to frighten him ? "

" It is even more diabolically subtle than that, Watson. Observe." He pointed to one end of the stick, where a white thread wrapped it round. " Do you remember what we found earlier?"

" Of course, a thread similar to that."

" Stand where we found that thread, Watson, and cast your gaze upward to the ceiling."

I obediently did so and perceived a small dark object against the white ceiling. " What is that?"

" It appears to be a small hook that has been fastened to the ceiling in some way. My surmise is that the hook was put in place, and the thread passed through it, and into the connecting bathroom through the fanlight which, as you can see, is slightly ajar. The Mace would be tied to the thread, and kept up close to the ceiling—you will observe that particular part of the room is hidden by the corner of the wardrobe from anyone lying in the bed. At a suitable time, the perpetrator would create some sort of disturbance which would ensure that Hareby awoke. I am sure that there are suitable implements in the bathroom to achieve that end. It would be easy enough to listen, provided the rain was not falling as you described to me earlier, and determine whether Hareby had, in fact, woken.

" Once it had been determined that he was no longer asleep, the Mace could be lowered, maybe to the accompaniment of some sort of sound intended to create terror. We were told that Hareby had some sort of obsession with the Mace. Imagine the effect of it being suspended in mid-air, with no apparent means of support. When I held it just now, were not my hands, and to a certain extent, my face, illuminated?"

" That is so."

" But the ingenuity of this scheme was that there was no-one visible. The perpetrator could listen for the effects that the vision of the Mace would have on the victim, and then, as

I deduce, release the thread, allowing the stick to drop to the floor, and incidentally allowing some of the phosphoric compound with which it is coated to fall onto the carpet."

" This all seems perfectly logical."

" It is indeed perfectly logical, because it occurred in the precise manner I am describing," he remarked severely. " Then comes the problem for the perpetrator of how to dispose of the Mace so that it will not be discovered. There would be a real risk of discovery if the Mace were to be carried outside the room into the passageway. Some servant or even a guest such as yourself might chance upon it. Added to which, it would have to be secreted somewhere after it had been carried out of the room.

" Concealing it somewhere within this room is out of the question. A servant would undoubtedly shortly discover it, and in any case, the time available would be brief. The answer is obvious. The executor of this plan ran into the room, snatched up the Mace and the thread, incidentally breaking the thread and leaving a small length on the carpet, flung open the curtains just enough to allow the casement to be opened, and thrust the Mace down into the creeper covering the wall, before closing the window. Maybe the perpetrator then heard the sound of approaching footsteps. In any event, it was necessary to make a hurried exit."

" This is miraculous, Holmes. How did you come to deduce all this ? "

" When I took Lady Hareby's hand at tea just now, it was obvious."

" You are accusing her of this ? "

" Naturally. Who else could it be ? The recent scratches along the length of her arm were sufficient proof. You will recall that I made enquiries about a cat, and received the answer that there was no cat in the house. The nature of the abrasions had caused me to doubt the existence of a cat or other animal's having caused them in any case, but it was necessary for me to eliminate that possibility.

" The slight injuries she had sustained were consistent with those caused by a thorn bush or some other kind of plant. The scratches were not regularly spaced in the way that those resulting from the claws of an animal might be. The conclusion was therefore that she had thrust her hand into some plant which had produced these results. Maybe they were the result of doing some work in the garden, but I noticed on my arrival that the gardens here are not extensive. In any case, she does not appear to be the kind of woman who would interest herself in that kind of activity.

" I had already deduced that some object, treated with a luminous preparation, had been suspended from the ceiling. That much was obvious from the thread and the spot of luminous phosphoric compound we discovered, was it not? The fanlight above the door being ajar was another clue, of course. The implication was that it was the Mace, given poor Hareby's nervous condition and obsession with such matters, and of course, the fact that the Mace had been removed from the cabinet. Seeing the curtain half-open in that exact position led me to the conclusion that I reached.

" The marks of the chair on the carpet were obviously made when the perpetrator stood upon it when fastening the hook to the ceiling. I think we can rule out Lord Darlington in this case. Firstly, he suffers from gout, as you are aware ; secondly, he has no motive for this action ; and thirdly, as you will have no doubt observed, his stature would prevent him from reaching the ceiling. Lady Hareby, on the other hand, is built on generous lines, at least with regard to her height, and even in her delicate condition, I would judge it perfectly possible for her to have done this. I think, do you not, we may eliminate any of the servants from suspicion here ? "

" You certainly seem to have solved this case remarkably quickly," I commented.

" By no means. I have deduced the method and the perpetrator of what may or may not be a crime – that is to say, the harming by indirect means of Lord Hareby. I confess I am somewhat at a loss to know under what section of the law that would merit prosecution. I am also relatively certain that we now know how the Mace and jewellery were removed from the cabinet, and I now believe we know the identity of the thief.

The next question is, of course, why would she benefit from such a course of action? And what was she hoping to achieve?"

"As to the second, have you not answered that already? His madness or his death, or at the very least, his incapacitation?"

"And what precisely would that accomplish? If the estate is entailed in the male line, the title would never pass to her in the event of Lord Darlington's death, should her husband be unable to inherit by reason of insanity, or death."

"But it could pass to her son, even if she were never to be awarded the estate," I objected. I recalled to Holmes her words spoken to me the previous night regarding the future of the Hall, and her presumed ownership of it and its contents.

"That is, assuming that her unborn child is a male," he retorted. "That would be similar to gambling on the toss of a coin. And if the coin comes down on the wrong side, there is no second chance possible if Lord Hareby is no longer here."

"Well, whatever her motive may be, are you going to confront her with her crimes?" I asked.

"That, Watson, depends to a large extent on the condition of Lord Hareby. I am sure we will soon receive word on his condition from the hospital, and should his condition prove to be serious, or, God forbid it, should he die as a result of this little game played by his wife, then I will have no hesitation whatsoever in pursuing this case with all the means at my disposal. If, however, the prognosis is good, and he recovers, I think that it will be best to let sleeping dogs lie, at least temporarily. You and I know the truth of this matter, and we may well make Lady Hareby aware of our knowledge, but at present I see little advantage in making the matter public if no lasting harm comes to Lord Hareby."

"And the Mace? When all is said and done, this was the reason why you were originally requested to come here."

"True. I think it should be returned to the place whence it was taken, do you not agree?" he said, smiling. "We will remove the traces of luminous compound with which it has been smeared, and restore it to something close to its original state, I think, before doing so. I will do so with the utmost care, given that this is a precious object to the family."

"Take care," I warned him. "I know that you are used to the hazards involved in handling chemical substances, but as you know, many compounds of phosphorus are dangerous and injurious to one's health."

"Thank you," he replied. "I was aware of the fact, naturally, but your reminder is welcome, even so. Please go down and explain that I am a little fatigued after my journey and I am resting, as I explained earlier. I will come downstairs presently."

 FOLLOWED his instructions, and spent the time pleasantly enough chatting with Lord Darlington about angling, Lady Hareby apparently pursuing her own interests in another room of the house. Like most practitioners of the gentle art, the Earl was full of tales regarding his past exploits, and a good hour or so was spent in this way before the gong for dinner sounded.

Holmes joined us in the drawing room before going into dinner. As we were on the point of entering the dining-room, Bouverie entered bearing a telegram addressed to Lord Darlington, who opened it and scanned its contents.

"Good news," he proclaimed. "This is a report from the hospital on poor Edgar's condition. It is necessarily brief, but it appears that his life is in no danger, and though he seems confused, he is in good spirits, and is recovering. There are a few words commending you, Dr. Watson, on your prompt action and efficacious treatment."

"Good news, indeed," echoed Lady Hareby, but her words lacked conviction, at least to my ears.

We went into dinner in a better frame of mind, and the meal was, as on the previous night, well-cooked. Holmes was at his most sociable, and attempted to lead the conversation into a variety of different paths, but his efforts fell flat. Again a pall seemed to have settled over the company, in this instance caused by the absence of Lord Hareby, while on the previous night it had been caused by his presence.

After dinner, Lady Hareby withdrew, and Lord Darlington produced a decanter of port. "For you two gentlemen," he explained. "My gout, alas, does not allow me to indulge. I feel a sorry invalid, I am afraid."

"One glass only for me," replied Holmes. "Before we retire, though, I would be grateful if you could open the cabinet from which the Mace was taken, so that I may examine the mechanism of the lock and the hinges."

"Why certainly, if you think it will be of any use," replied Lord Darlington. "I can do that whenever you are ready."

"There is no time like the present," replied Holmes, draining his glass. I confess I was somewhat irritated by this, since I was enjoying the noble liquor, but at the same time I had a good idea of what Holmes had in mind, and I was keenly anticipating what was to come.

"Since you wish it," answered Lord Darlington and, rising, led the way into the library. "The Bramah lock, as you observe, and the single key to the lock is on my watch-chain here." He fitted the key to the lock and, as before, the door of the cabinet creaked open. "Now, as you will see, the interior of the cabinet is fitted with shelves, and the Mace used to repose on—" He broke off with a startled cry. "Good Lord, Mr.

Holmes! This is astounding!" He turned to Holmes and myself, his face suffused with a mixture of shock and delight.

"What has happened?" asked Holmes, innocently.

"The Mace seems to have returned! By what means and when, I do not know, but it is there now."

I did not trust myself to speak, knowing what had happened, but Holmes spoke to Lord Darlington. "Perhaps it was never missing, and you overlooked it when you first inspected the cabinet and discovered that the jewellery had been taken?"

"No, that is not possible," replied Lord Darlington. "As I explained to you, the Mace was kept in the cabinet, reposing on a red velvet cushion, and that cushion is now missing. I confess, Mr. Holmes, I am almost inclined to believe in the magical properties of the Mace. My daughter-in-law must know of this. Would one of you gentlemen be kind enough to fetch her?"

I volunteered for the task, and discovered Lady Hareby in the drawing-room.

"Why, Dr. Watson," she greeted me. "I was beginning to think that I had lost all my charm for the gentlemen. Will you join me?" patting the space on the sofa beside her.

"As it happens, Lord Darlington has requested that you join him and Mr. Holmes in the library. I believe that he has something of interest that he wishes to show to you."

"Oh, very well," she replied, with a bad grace. "Give me your arm, if you would, John." I blushed a little to hear my Christian name being bandied about so freely by this woman, but complied with her request.

I fancied she was holding my arm a little tighter than was necessary as we made our way to the library, but that was nothing compared to the pressure with which she gripped me when we entered the library, and she beheld her father-in-law proudly displaying the Mace. She stumbled and nearly collapsed, and were it not for my arm, I believe she would have fallen to the ground.

"Wonderful, is it not, my dear?" exclaimed the Earl, apparently oblivious of her state.

"Yes, wonderful indeed," she replied. "What a piece of luck. The shock has made me weak. Doctor, will you help me to a chair?" I hastened to seat her comfortably in one of the library chairs, from which she gazed at Holmes and myself with wonder, mixed with a certain animosity, in her eyes.

"Your child will be safe," the Earl told her, but she appeared to be somewhat less than reassured by his words. "Well," he continued, seemingly having no eyes for anything but the Mace, which he replaced in the cabinet and locked it. "Bless me," he muttered to himself. "Truly miraculous." He turned to us. "Well, this excitement has fatigued me. With your permission, I will retire and bid you a very good night." He shuffled out of the room, and we heard the door of the next room being opened and closed.

"Well, Mr. Holmes," said Lady Hareby, in a low but angry voice. "I suppose that you consider yourself to be a clever man?"

"I know that to be the case," he replied.

"How much have you guessed?" she enquired.

"I consider that I know most of the facts of the case. Guesswork was not a significant factor."

"And what do you propose doing about it?" she asked, coolly.

"Why, nothing at present," he replied, "given the news we received from the hospital before dinner. It would appear that your husband will suffer no lasting infirmity."

"And I am certain that even if he had suffered such, even your keen brain would be unable to discover the precise statute under which I could be charged." Her tone was now openly mocking.

"True," Holmes acknowledged. "I perceive you have been taking lessons in the law from Sir Godfrey Wrigley."

She flushed slightly. "It is no business of yours from whom I derive my opinions on the law," she retorted. "In any case, I take it that you propose to do nothing? I am a free woman as far as you are concerned?"

"Free, but consider yourself under my scrutiny." Holmes drew himself to his full height, and stood in front of her chair, his eyes boring down into hers. "I should warn you that those with more cunning and cleverness than you possess have attempted to best me, and they have failed. I advise you to cease from attempting any further tricks of the type that you have recently played. Watson and I will stay in this room tonight, to prevent a further theft of the Mace, and I will inform Lord Darlington in the morning before our departure for London regarding the means used to remove it. He will then be free to make whatever assumptions he may choose regarding the identity of the thief."

"I suppose you expect my gratitude?"

"It is immaterial to me as to whether you care to bestow it or not. I would, however, myself be grateful were you to confirm one point for me."

"That being?"

"The reason for the removal of the jewellery."

"I would be interested to know your theories, Mr. Holmes." The mocking smile was still there, and I had the sensation of being present at a duel between two masters of fencing, elegant in their style, but deadly in the execution of their art.

"Firstly, I believe that the jewels were taken partly in order to divert attention from the removal of the Mace."

"Very good, but somewhat obvious, do you not think?"

" Perhaps so," Holmes admitted. I might also surmise that they were removed in order to provide funds for closing the mouths of those who might talk about matters that the thief would sooner not have noised about town."

Lady Hareby smiled at Holmes. " A most ingenious theory, Mr. Holmes, but I am happy to tell you that you are incorrect in your surmise. I will, of course, refrain from informing you of the true reason. And with that, gentlemen..." She made as if to rise, and I assisted her to her feet. " I bid you a very good night," she concluded. " I hope that you sleep well in each other's company." She made a mocking curtsey and swept out of the room.

I turned to Holmes, feeling a faint smile spread across my face. " It seems I am destined to spend another night out of the comfort of my luxurious bed upstairs," I remarked. " I am intrigued by why you decided to let that woman go free, though."

Holmes yawned. " It would be too tedious to explain at present," he replied. " In any case, I do not regard her as being free while she is under my eye, and trust me, Watson, I intend to keep her under observation."

With that, we made our arrangements, and settled down for the night.

 dangerous woman," remarked Sherlock Holmes, as we sat in a first-class carriage making our way back to London, a cheque for a large sum of money reposing in Holmes' pocket-book.

Earlier that morning Holmes had demonstrated to Lord Darlington how the cabinet containing the Mace could be accessed from the side, through the cavity left by removing the wooden panel. Lord Darlington had been astonished and horrified at the ease with which Holmes had removed the Mace, leaving not a trace of his activities, and had immediately given orders for a workman to be summoned from working on the estate to ensure that this method of access was permanently disabled in the future.

However, Holmes had resolutely refused to provide details of who had purloined the items, leaving Lord Darlington, as he had remarked the previous evening, to draw his own conclusions regarding this.

"A dangerous woman," he repeated, filling his pipe and lighting it. "Singularly devoid of conscience and blessed, or cursed, depending on one's point of view, with considerable intelligence. Your strength of mind in resisting her advances to you is to be highly commended," he said to me. "Nothing but trouble would have ensued had you succumbed to her considerable charms, I am convinced."

"I confess that I feel myself relieved by this. What, though, do you think was her secondary object in purloining the jewellery?"

"I have no definite thoughts on the matter. To repeat one of my favourite maxims, it is a mistake to theorise before one has all the facts available. Otherwise one tends to twist the facts to suit the theory, rather than the other way around."

"Are you not somewhat concerned about her, though?"

"I have grave concerns about the whole tribe at Hareby. Lord Darlington seems to be in thrall to childish superstition, and seems to be incapable of controlling his own family. His son—well, you have seen his son, and I have not, but from your description, it appears that he will be totally unfit to take over the title and the responsibilities. And then we have his wife, whom I believe we both agree is riding for a fall."

"It is not a pleasant prospect."

"We are free, at least for the present, of the influence of the Darlingtons, I think. I can now return to that problem presented to me the other day by François le Villard, which promises to provide a respite from the tedium of everyday life." So saying, he closed his eyes, and entered a wordless reverie, while continuing to fill the compartment with the acrid fumes of his coarse tobacco.

THE DISAPPEARANCE
OF LORD HAREBY

Chapter X
Bouverie,
The Butler

T was about a month later that we had an unexpected visitor. Holmes had just completed one or two somewhat delicate cases that had required tact and diplomacy for their solution, and was taking what I considered to be a well-earned break from his labours, but which he regarded with impatience. We were sitting round the table in the centre of the room, working on updating the large scrapbook that Holmes named his "Index" with newspaper cuttings.

Some of the subjects that Holmes selected were of obvious interest and had a connection with his work. Such items included reports of police court proceedings, reports of unsolved crimes, or some reports of unusual events. I failed to perceive the reasoning that led him to clip out and file a report on copper production in Chile, for example.

"I cannot speak more of this," he said, in answer to my query. "My brother Mycroft has an interest in this matter, and he is too indolent to find the information for himself. His skills lie in the tying together of threads, rather than the discovery of them."

I was aware of the shadowy position of Mycroft Holmes in the British government, and contented myself with this enigmatic pronouncement.

As we were seated at our task, Mrs. Hudson knocked on the door and announced that Holmes had a visitor.

"Well, show him up, Mrs. Hudson," said Holmes. "Why did you not bring him with you?"

"Well, I wanted to warn you, especially you, Doctor, that he doesn't seem to be in a good way at all. If you want my opinion, Mr. Holmes, he's more in need of a doctor than your services, to look at him."

"Show him in, anyway, if you would. Really!" he exclaimed, as the door closed behind her. "'If you want my opinion,' indeed. When I require the opinion of my landlady, I will ask for it. Until that time … "

The rest of his tirade was curtailed by a knock at the door. The person who entered the room appeared familiar, but it was a few seconds before I recognised him, so distorted was his face with strain and worry. I assisted him with his overcoat and hat, and sat him in a chair near the fire.

"You appear unwell, Bouverie," I addressed him. "What, may I ask, are you doing in London?"

"I came here special to see Mr. Holmes, I did." In his agitation, his diction and his accent, which I had noted during my sojourn at Hareby as those of a superior servant, appeared to have slipped a little. "Since I had to come up to London today on another errand, it seemed to me that it would be a good move for me to come and see Mr. Holmes here, seeing as how he put things right a few weeks back. Not that I'm not glad to see you, Doctor. My nerves are all shot to pieces. It's the wailing and the howling all night that's doing it."

"Here, pull yourself together, man," I told him sternly, "and drink this," pouring him a stiff brandy-and-water.

"Thank you, sir," he replied, taking the glass from me with a shaking hand, and lifting it to his mouth.

"Have you been drinking, Bouverie?" I asked him.

"No sir, I hardly ever drink, and I haven't touched a drop these past few days, I swear to you, though I confess I've been sorely tempted."

"Come, man," said Holmes. "Pull yourself together and tell us what is distressing you in this way. You are hearing strange noises?"

The butler took a pull at his drink, and paused. "Yes, sir. At first, Mrs. Bouverie and I thought it was the baby." As the colour returned to his cheeks, his speech became more composed.

"The baby?" Holmes enquired.

"Yes, sir. I am sorry. I would have thought you might have been told about it. Lady Hareby was delivered of a baby boy two weeks ago. Funny little mite he is, though I suppose I shouldn't be saying that, but good as gold. Hardly ever lets out a peep or a whimper.

"But the last week, we've been hearing an uncanny wailing and howling which sounds like a baby, but whenever Mrs. Bouverie has looked in on the nursery, the little one was fast asleep." Bouverie leaned forward, his elbows on his knees, and his voice shrank to a hoarse whisper. "Mr. Holmes, do you believe in the Mace of Succession? I know you have heard the story, because of your visit a month ago."

"Do I believe in it?" my friend replied, smiling. "I believe in its physical existence, naturally, since I have seen and handled the object in question. If you are asking whether I believe the tales and superstitions attached to it, the answer is that I do not. What is your reason for asking?"

"Well, sir, I don't say that I believe in it myself, but at the same time, I feel it would be foolish of me to deny the truth of the matter entirely, if you take my meaning. The thing is, sir, that there is this tradition in the family of removing the coin from the Mace, as you probably know, and it's not been done yet, even after the baby's been with us for nearly two weeks now. It may sound somewhat daft to you," (I smiled inwardly at this use of the word, which was common enough among the Fusiliers with whom I had served, but was less frequently used in the south of the country) "but the sounds we are hearing, you might say that they are almost like the cries of the spirit of a dead child."

"That sounds like an extremely fanciful description, if you will forgive my saying so, Mr. Bouverie," replied Holmes. "One with which I personally would find it hard to agree.

From where do these strange sounds appear to be coming, and is there any pattern to their timing? Do they always come at a certain time of day, for example?"

"There seems to be no rhyme or reason to it, sir, as far as the time of day is concerned. Sometimes it happens in the middle of the night, and sometimes it's in broad daylight. Usually it doesn't go on for more than about five minutes at a time, but last night was something terrible, and it was that which made me come and talk to you about it, given that I was in London anyway on an errand for his Lordship. As to where they're coming from, that's another mystery in itself. They seem to be coming from the next room sometimes, but when we go in there, no-one is to be seen, and the crying noises stop. I think on every occasion we have heard the sounds, we have been upstairs on the first floor, or in our room on the second floor at the back of the Hall."

"Most singular," said Holmes. "I can understand why you are ascribing a supernatural origin to these sounds, but it is not an explanation that commends itself to me. Do you have anything else to tell me about this? Have you kept a record of the times and occasions when you hear these noises?" Bouverie indicated with a shake of his head that he had not done so. "Very well. I would like you, when you return to the Hall, to commence keeping such a record. Please note the exact time when you first noticed the sounds, how long they continue, where you are when you hear them, and from where they appear to be coming. If you will send me these reports as often as possible, this will be extremely useful."

"I will do my best to carry out your wishes in this, Mr. Holmes," replied the butler. "Naturally, I do not feel it is my place to offer you an invitation to the Hall, but it would ease my mind if you were come to Hareby and see and hear for yourself what's going on there."

"As you say, it would be inappropriate for me to visit at

your request," agreed Holmes, "but I can perceive some merit in your suggestion. You have said that you and your wife are disturbed by these sounds. What of the other inhabitants of the house?"

"Well, sir, among the servants, the housemaids are the ones who have heard it in the daytime, since they are upstairs more. Sally Crowthorpe, who found Lord Hareby that morning—I think you spoke to her, sir," addressed to me, "said that she was going to give notice, as it shattered her nerves, she said."

"But she has not done so?"

"She has not yet left the Hall," admitted Bouverie. "My wife talked to her and persuaded her to stay, but she may change her mind at any time, I fear. The other housemaids are also fearful, and the cook and the kitchen-maids perhaps a little less, for what reason I do not know."

"And what of the family?"

"Lord Darlington, if I may speak frankly, is somewhat hard of hearing, as I am sure you are aware, and he has made no remark to me about this. Nor has he given any sign that he has perceived the sounds. Lady Hareby, when my wife asked her if she had been inconvenienced by the cries, she said that she had heard nothing. Lord Hareby ... " and here the good fellow shook his head.

"Lord Hareby is out of hospital, then?" I asked. "I am glad to hear it."

"So are we all, sir, but I fear that he is not much longer for this world. I'm not meaning to make any guesses, seeing that I'm no doctor, sir, but he seems to be very weak and there doesn't seem to be a lot of life left in him. Most of the time he's just lying in his bed, and when he does get up, he looks tired out, before he's even lifted a finger. He used to enjoy his walks around the estate, but he's not set a foot outside the Hall since he came back from the hospital."

Holmes' next question was rather unexpected, both to me,

and, so it seemed, to Bouverie. " What are his feelings regarding the birth of his son? " asked my friend. " Has that event not inspired him with life? "

" Now that's another strange thing, Mr. Holmes. He's been told that his son has been born, but he doesn't seem in the least interested in the event. In fact, he has seen his son only once, to the best of my knowledge, since he returned from the hospital."

" Curious, most curious." Holmes appeared to be lost in thought for a minute before he looked up and spoke to the butler. " The ritual with the Mace has yet to take place, you say? " The other nodded. " Has any date been fixed, do you know? "

" No, sir. The old Earl is keen to get it done, of course, because as I am sure he told you when he recounted the legend, the penny must be removed from the Mace within seven days of the birth of the child and before the boy is christened. But at the same time, he seems to feel that he should not perform the Ritual until Lord Hareby feels well enough to attend." He coughed discreetly. " It is not that his Lordship takes me into his confidence in these matters, you understand, but after many years in his service, I feel that I have some understanding of his wishes in matters such as these."

" I am sure that you do," Holmes assured him. " It may well be that I will come to the area, and base myself near the Hall in order to investigate these events, which sound more than a little disturbing, it is true. In that event, I will make you aware of my presence in the area, and I am certain that I will be able to come to some conclusions regarding your mysterious noises."

" Thank you, sir," said the fellow, donning his coat and hat and leaving us.

"confess to feeling some sympathy for the man," said Holmes, as the sound of our visitor's footsteps retreated down the stairs.

"Maybe he is to be pitied in some ways," I admitted, "but I would feel somewhat more well-disposed towards him were he not stealing from his master."

"Why do you say that?" asked Holmes.

"Is there any reason you can consider why he should be carrying a case of silver spoons or some such plate in his overcoat pocket?"

"Bravo, Watson! So you also noticed that, but I fear you have placed the wrong interpretation on the worthy Bouverie's actions. The fact that the case was in his pocket and, as you say, is of a type that almost certainly contains plate of some kind, would seem to mark him down as a thief, would it not? Especially since he has come from the North up to London to dispose of the booty."

"That was my assumption," I agreed.

"What you failed to observe, obviously, was the receipt from Asprey's protruding from his waistcoat pocket. From the scuffed appearance of the case, and the fact that it carried the Darlington coat of arms, we may conclude that he had taken some of the Hall silver to that shop earlier for repair, and was now collecting it. He did, after all, inform us that he had business in London, and I hardly think he would have informed us of that fact if that business were against the law."

"What do you make of his story about the noises produced by the phantom baby?"

"Traditionally, butlers are often accused of drunkenness, thanks to their free access to the wine cellars of the houses where they are employed, but I do not feel that to be the case here. I believe, since he mentions various other members of the staff also hearing these noises, that the sounds are actually occurring, and are not merely the figments of his imagination, alcoholically stimulated or otherwise."

"I spoke with the housemaid whom he mentioned, Sally Crowthorpe, when I was making enquiries about Lord Hareby on the morning of his illness," I informed Holmes. "She struck me as being a very sensible and level-headed kind of woman, though obviously when I talked with her, she was somewhat distraught as the result of finding Lord Hareby in that condition."

"So in your opinion, Watson, we can assume that the sounds that are filling the ears of Mr. and Mrs. Bouverie are real, and are not merely the products of an overactive imagination?"

"I would say so."

"I also. There are strange doings afoot. I am demanding much of you, Watson, but I wish to be left alone for a few hours. Have the goodness to leave me, and pass the word to Mrs. Hudson that I am not to be disturbed until this evening. When you return, we will sally forth and sample the delights at Alberti's or any other establishment that takes your fancy. I will foot the bill, naturally, being at present in a state of some affluence as the result of a trifling case that resulted in a financial reward out of all proportion to the time I spent in solving it."

There was nothing for it when Holmes gave orders such as this, albeit framed as requests, but for me to remove myself from his presence and take myself elsewhere. It was a pleasant day, and I amused myself with a walk in the Park, observing the passers-by and applying to them the principles of deduction that I had learned from Holmes. I was puzzled by one young man, who appeared to be of good birth, and who was dressed fashionably, but whose ears, I noticed, were somewhat incongruously pierced for earrings. He had a curious white mark on his forehead, as if he had been splashed with some liquid. His eyes were constantly darting about him, but appeared to be fixed in my direction more than in any other. He took note of the fact that I was observing him, whereupon he moved away from me quickly before I was able to study him further.

As the dusk started to draw in, I retraced my steps to Baker-street, where Mrs. Hudson greeted me.

"Maybe you can take this up to him since you've returned, Doctor," she said, extending an envelope to me. "I didn't want to be the one to disturb him, even though it is a telegram."

"Thank you. I am sure you have done the right thing," I smiled at her, and climbed to our rooms.

The room was thick with blue pipe smoke, and through the haze, I could see Sherlock Holmes lying on the sofa, his pipe clenched between his teeth, gazing fixedly at the opposite wall.

"Have you solved the problem?" I asked him, and fell to coughing violently. "This atmosphere is really intolerable. Allow me to open the window." I suited the action to the words, and the smoke in the room was gradually replaced by fresh air.

"The Darlington problem?" he replied. "No, I have not, I fear. There are too many possible solutions, if I base my reasoning on only what we have been told. If I am to solve the case, we must attend in person. I did, however, settle to my own satisfaction that some of the themes of the polyphonic motets of Lassus are at least in part derived from the originals by Palestrina, but that is hardly germane to the matter at hand. Is that telegram addressed to me, by the by?" he broke off, and extended his hand, into which I placed the envelope.

"Well, this ranks as coincidence, I would say," he remarked, scanning the telegram. "Lord Darlington informs us that the Ritual of the Mace will take place tomorrow afternoon, and extends an invitation to both of us to attend."

"Indeed, coincidence."

" What time does the sleeper train that you took with Lord Darlington depart from King's Cross?   Maybe we will forego our little Italian expedition tonight. With luck, we will be able to justify a true celebration when we return."

Holmes scribbled out a telegram accepting the invitation, and requesting that we be met at Berwick station on our arrival and gave instructions for its dispatch before we packed our bags and started for the terminus.

CHAPTER XI
HANSHAW, THE COACHMAN

N arrival at Berwick station, we were met by the coachman, Hanshaw. He raised his cap to us as he recognised me.

"Glad to see you again, Doctor," he exclaimed with what appeared to be genuine pleasure, "and you too, sir. I am guessing you must be Mr. Sherlock Holmes? I wished I'd had the pleasure of driving you to and from the Hall on your last visit. There are some questions I would like to ask you, if you don't mind talking on the way to the Hall, sir?"

I was pleased to see Holmes in a genial mood. Often when approached by those who wanted to treat him as some sort of celebrity, he became reserved and aloof, which had left him in some circles with a reputation for haughtiness and unfriendliness.

"I will be happy to listen to your questions," he said, smiling. "Maybe I can answer them, Mr.—?"

"Hanshaw. Earnest Hanshaw. Thank you very much, sir. Are these cases all of your luggage, Mr. Holmes and Dr. Watson?"

I assured him that they were, and informed him that we would take tea in the station refreshment room while he loaded the trap, inviting him to join us when he had completed the task.

"A talkative fellow," remarked Holmes, "and not one who seems to be in awe of those that society tells him are his superiors."

"Lord Darlington seems to repose great trust in him," I replied. "When I travelled this way last time, he and Hanshaw seemed to be almost like old friends, rather than master and man."

"That is good to know," remarked Holmes, as the tea and toast we had ordered made their appearance. He munched thoughtfully. "He may be able to tell us some more about Lord Darlington's state of mind."

At that moment, Hanshaw entered the room, and asked permission to join us.

" Thank you, gentlemen," he said, doffing his cap. " It's a cold drive from the Hall of a morning, and a drop of tea's welcome at this hour."

" I am sure it is," agreed Holmes. " Now, you wanted to ask me some questions? " Hanshaw nodded in agreement, his mouth at that moment being full of toast. " I am happy to do so," went on Holmes, " as long as you answer some of my questions in return."

" That seems like a fair bargain, sir," said the other, the toast having now been disposed of. " Though I'm not so sure that the answers I give you to your questions will be as interesting as the answers you give to my questions."

Holmes smiled. " You might be surprised at what interests me, Hanshaw. Your first question, then? "

" Well, sir, I know you've seen and done a lot of things, but … do you believe in ghosts? "

Instead of laughing outright, which I feared Holmes might do, he appeared to consider the matter seriously. " That's a very good question. I do believe that people see and hear things that aren't there in a physical sense—that is, we are unable to touch or feel them—but I cannot believe that they are spirits of the departed. Speaking for myself, I have never seen a ghost that couldn't be explained in some way other than that of a departed spirit."

" I see, sir."

" I suggest to you, Hanshaw, that you have a reason for asking, and it is connected with sounds that some at the Hall have been hearing over the past week or so."

The other started somewhat at Holmes' words. " Why yes, that's right, sir. Did his Lordship tell you something about this? "

" No, it was Bouverie, the butler who informed me."

" He had to go to London yesterday to take care of some of the silver. I know because it was me who drove him to the station and fetched him back again. He visited you then ? "

" That is correct," said Holmes. " It seems that the questions I have and the questions you have are directed towards the same end, then. Excellent. Have you heard the noises yourself ? "

" No sir, I have not. I do not work inside the Hall, and I only enter it to eat my meals in the kitchen downstairs. I sleep above the stables, which you may remember are some distance from the Hall itself. It's my young lady Edith, who is one of the house-maids, who's told me all about it. I call her my 'young lady', but at my age, anything below fifty is young, if you take my meaning, sir. The sound is like a baby wailing, is what she told me, but there's only one baby in the house, and when they go in to look at him, he's sleeping there quiet as a little dormouse."

" And is there any particular time of day that this happens ? " asked Holmes.

" She said to me that it seems to happen more at night. She shares a room at night with two of the other house-maids, Sally Crowthorpe and Harriet Bell, and the two of them daft women got themselves nearly hysterical one night, she told me. My Edith has got her head screwed on and told them to pull themselves together and stop their blethering, but she told me they nearly walked out of the Hall, never to come back."

" Well, your young lady sounds sensible enough," said Holmes, smiling. " Since she has heard the noise, and does not think it's a ghost, what are her ideas about it ? "

" She thinks it's no more than wind whistling down the chimneys. She may be right at that, since there's a powerful wind comes in from the east some nights, and the Hall's exposed on that side. She did say that it sounded like a baby, though, more than the wind."

" Our imagination plays strange tricks on us sometimes, as you know. And I am sure you know that your mind can change things into what you want them to be."

" True enough, sir. So you think it is just the wind?"

" I cannot say that is definitely the case, but I think it more than likely, from what you have just told me."

" There are those who are going around saying it's all to do with the Mace, and that if the penny had been thrown down the well, they wouldn't be hearing these sounds of crying now."

" You know the story of the Mace, then?"

" Of course, sir. It's one of the local legends, and there's no getting away from it in these parts."

" But you do not believe in it yourself, do you? A sensible rational man like yourself?"

The question obviously embarrassed Hanshaw. On the one hand, he seemed to wish to impress Holmes, whom he obviously looked up to and respected, with his rationality. At the same time there appeared to be some deeply held belief that conflicted with what he believed to be true. At length he burst out with, " I can't rightly say. There are too many stories for me to disbelieve it entirely, but wouldn't you say that it seems somewhat fanciful in the nineteenth century?"

" I would agree that it seems fanciful," said Holmes. " As fanciful as the stories of ghosts."

" If that's the case," persisted Hanshaw, " then why does a man like Lord Darlington, who's been in the government and so on, believe in it the way he does? I don't understand that part of it at all."

" Well, if you did, Hanshaw, you would be a famous man," smiled Holmes. " We do not understand all the little twists and turns of human nature, try as we might. It is sad to reflect that we have an understanding of the stars and of the distant planets, but we are still unable to look inside our own souls and determine what the guiding principles might be in there."

"True enough, sir. Now, if you gentlemen are finished with your breakfasts, may I suggest that we start for the Hall?"

"Very good," agreed Holmes. "By the by," he asked as we strolled to the waiting trap, "do you know anything of Lord Hareby's condition?"

"He's much better than he was, sir," replied Hanshaw. "Indeed, he rose from his bed and took a turn around the stable-yard yesterday morning. It was that which decided Lord Darlington to perform the Ritual. I think he felt it wouldn't be right to do it without the father of the baby being present."

"If half the tales concerning Lady Hareby are true," Holmes commented to me in an almost inaudible undertone, "finding the true father of the child would be an interesting task indeed."

I ignored this, instead remarking aloud to Hanshaw, "I am glad to hear of the improvement in Lord Hareby's condition."

"He looked very weak when I saw him yesterday, though, sir. I had only seen him the once after he went into the hospital, and that was when I brought him back from there."

"Did you speak to him?" I asked.

"No, sir. He always used to have a good word for everybody, but yesterday he looked so miserable that no-one had the heart to disturb him. He was all wrapped up in himself, it seemed, and not in any kind of mood to talk to anyone else."

"Was he alone? Was his wife with him?"

By now we were trotting through the streets of Berwick. Hanshaw was looking straight in front of him, guiding the trap, and Holmes and I were unable to see his face, but his voice showed his emotion. "No, sir, his wife was not with him. In fact, we have hardly seen his wife outside the Hall since the baby was born."

"That is perfectly in order," I said. "As a doctor, I generally forbid my female patients from leaving their beds for some days after childbirth."

I watched the back of his head move from side to side as he shook his head. "She was up and about the day after, so my Edith tells me. Dr. Brendell tried to prevent her, but," he chuckled drily, "you've met Dr. Brendell and you've met Lady Hareby. Meaning no disrespect to him or to her, but I think you can guess who would win that argument."

"I am not certain you should be talking of your employer in that way," Holmes said to him. "But what you are telling us is most interesting, even so."

"Begging your pardon, sir, but Lady Hareby's not my employer, and I pray to God that she never will be."

Much to my relief, for the conversation was verging on dangerous ground, Holmes did not pursue this topic, but sat back, scanning the rough moors that surrounded us. "Wild country here," he remarked after a while. "Are you a native of these parts?"

"It is pretty rough, sir," came the answer. "The winters are cold, and yes, I was born and bred here. I remember one winter when there was ice on the pond all the time from October through to April. But it is beautiful country, sir. I wouldn't live anywhere else for anything."

E arrived at the Hall drive and turned in. As we trotted along the driveway, a distraught figure ran towards us. As he approached, we could make out the features of Bouverie, the butler.

"Mr. Holmes!" he shouted to us when he came within earshot. "Mr. Holmes!"

" Please draw up, Hanshaw," Holmes requested him, but the coachman had already anticipated this request.

The butler looked up at us, his chest heaving, and his face red with the exertion of his having run to meet us.

" Take your time," Holmes told him kindly. " Hanshaw, can this trap take another person ? "

" No matter, I will walk," I told Holmes, springing from the trap. " It will do me good to stretch my legs after the train journey." I also welcomed the chance to breathe the fresh country air, something I believe I always appreciated more than did Holmes, who always appeared to be somewhat out of his element when removed from the smoke and fogs of London.

" Thank you, sir," said Bouverie, panting, as he took my place in the trap next to Holmes. " I'm not as young as I was, sir, as I have just discovered." He smiled ruefully.

" Now, what is the matter ? " Holmes asked him.

" Well, sir, it's Lord Hareby. He's disappeared."

" What ? " I cried, but at that moment the trap set off in the direction of the Hall, and I was left behind, with a distance of about half a mile to cover on foot—no hardship, since the weather was warm and no rain was falling. I strode along the drive towards the Hall, digesting the news that Bouverie had imparted. The scenery surrounding me could not be ignored, despite my worries, and I found myself amazed once more by the variety and beauty of our English countryside.

As I walked along, my eye was caught by a shining object in the long grass by the side of the drive. If it had not been for the fact that it caught the rays of the sun, which appeared from behind a cloud at the precise moment that I walked past it, it would almost certainly have gone unnoticed by me.

I stooped to pick it up, and saw that it was a handsome hunter watch, in what appeared to be a silver mount, with the chain still attached. The back was engraved with an inscription, " To E from E", together with a date, and I had no difficulty in assigning the names " Edgar" and " Elizabeth" to the initials.

Given what Bouverie had just informed us regarding Lord Hareby's disappearance, I immediately endeavoured to apply the methods I had learned from Holmes to investigate the situation, with some success (if I may be permitted a certain amount of self-congratulation).

I took care not to disturb the ground around where I had discovered the watch, but it was clear that there were footprints leading from the drive to the site of the watch, some two yards from the road, which then continued towards the Hall. There was no doubt regarding the direction of travel away from the drive, back towards the Hall, as in one or two places, the imprint of a foot in the soft earth could be clearly discerned.

I followed the trail, and after a few yards, came across a tie and a collar lying in the grass. I determined not to touch them, but continued following the trail of footprints and crushed grass, discovering further garments strewn along the way. It appeared to me that the poor fellow had lost his wits, and had run through the grass (for at several places where the footprints were clearly visible, only the imprint of the toes was to be seen), stopping at intervals to remove his clothes. Eventually, the footprints re-joined the driveway near the Hall, and it proved impossible to follow the trail any further. I ran to the front door of the Hall, which opened as I mounted the steps, and I collided with Holmes, who was just leaving the house.

" You appear to have been running," he observed. " Why the excitement ? Will you join me in my search for Lord Hareby ? "

I explained what I had just discovered, and Holmes was instantly alert. " Good man, Watson," he exclaimed. " I would surely have discovered these things myself, but you have undoubtedly saved time. Show me first where you picked up the trail."

As we walked towards the place where I had discovered the watch, Holmes informed me of what Bouverie had told him as they drove to the Hall in the trap. Lord Hareby had apparently woken, dressed himself and come down to breakfast, for only the second time since he had returned from the hospital. His father had expressed his delight, which was increased when the young man announced his intention of taking a constitutional along the driveway to the gates of the park and then returning.

His father had suggested that he be attended by one of the servants, but his son had shrugged off any such offer of assistance, stating quite bluntly that he preferred to make his own way, and was not in need of any help.

Bouverie had watched him set off from the Hall, and confirmed that although Lord Hareby was walking slowly along the drive, he appeared to be steady and confident in his gait. The butler then returned to his duties, but when he next looked out, some ten minutes later, Lord Hareby was nowhere to be seen. He continued gazing at the point where he had last seen his master's son, but there was no sign of anyone there.

He called out to one of the gardeners, who followed Lord Hareby's supposed path, but who reported on his return that he had been unable to see anything. Bouverie then espied the carriage bearing Holmes and myself, and ran down to meet it, guessing the identity of its occupants.

" Does Lord Darlington know that his son is missing? "

" Bouverie is endeavouring to keep the news from him. Apparently the old man is in a nervous state, and Bouverie has concerns for his health."

" And Lady Hareby? "

" She is apparently in the nursery with her child. She has

not been informed of her husband's disappearance, which may, after all, be purely temporary and no cause for real concern."

" I hope you are correct in that latter assumption."

" I, too. Ah." Holmes stopped. " This is where you found the watch, I take it? That showed excellent foresight."

I had previously marked the spot where the watch had lain in the grass by planting my stick into the ground by the side of the carriageway, and tying my handkerchief to it to assist in finding it again, and it was to this that Holmes was referring.

" These are your footprints, obviously, from the square-capped boots," remarked my friend, dropping to one knee and scrutinising the trampled grass. " And the watch lay here. Ah yes, tiptoe, tiptoe," he murmured, crawling forward on his hands and knees, following the trail. And the collar and tie are where you found them? You did not touch them? " I confirmed this. " These were not simply removed, Watson. These were ripped off in haste. Observe, the material of the tie has actually been torn by the force with which the tie was removed and the collar has been damaged by the stud as a result of the haste with which it was removed."

" He removed it himself? Or was the action performed by another? " I asked.

" I hardly think another was involved. There is only one set of prints. He was alone, running, and then he stopped, ripped off his collar and tie, and proceeded." Holmes rose to his feet and stooped to examine the grass. " Running again, and now stopped, and here is his coat. Look here, the sleeves are reversed, the lining is ripped, presumably where it caught on his cuff-links, and all indications are that this too was flung off in a frenzy. And now the running again. It appears that he was like a man possessed."

I felt a shudder running down my spine at those words. " Holmes," I said to him, " I would much prefer that you used other words to describe his state."

" I do not mean that he was possessed by any spirit or any-thing of that nature," replied Holmes. " Rather that he was not in his right mind, and that something, almost certainly of a physical nature rather than a spiritual, had seized his poor body and was driving it on in an unnatural fashion."

" Could not his mania have caused this ? "

" Possibly, but look here." By now we had reached the shirt that had been thrown on the ground. " What do you make of this ? "

" It is spittle, I would hazard," I replied, examining a stain on the sleeve of the garment. " It appears to be mixed with mucus and blood."

" I agree. There was no history of consumption ? "

" Not of which I am aware."

" I think we would have been informed had that been the case. What makes a man tear off his clothes, run like a fiend through the fields, and produce these fluids ? "

" I cannot say."

" Some drug administered to him, I would guess, the exact composition of which I cannot be certain. Let us follow the trail and see where it leads."

As we proceeded, it became obvious to Holmes, as it had to me earlier, that our quarry was by now completely naked, hav-ing divested himself of all his clothes. The trail ended at the driveway, and even Holmes' skills were unable to take the trail further. " Observe two spots of blood here," he remarked to me, and cast around in vain for further evidence.

" A dog ? " I suggested.

" A good thought there, Watson. Ah, but if we only had Toby, whose services we employed in the case of Jonathan Small and the Sign of the Four," replied Holmes. " But it is useless to wish for the impossible, and we must make do with what we have." So saying, he set off, walking briskly in the di-rection of the stables.

" Where are you going? "

" To talk to Hanshaw. He will know if there is a dog suitable for our purposes."

Hanshaw, when we discovered him, and had explained the situation to him, was immediately helpful. " There's Bosker," he told us. " One of the foxhounds. He is a little lame, and he does not go out with the Hunt any more, but he has the best nose in the kennels. If you two gentlemen will wait here, I will go and fetch him."

Holmes rubbed his hands together briskly. " It is always a pleasure to find someone as quick-witted and obliging as our man here. I confess to feeling more sanguine already."

N a few minutes Hanshaw returned, leading a hound which, as had been explained, limped a little, and which sniffed with interest at Holmes' trouser leg when introduced. For his part, Holmes, who typically displayed an indifference towards animals, appeared taken with Bosker, patting his head and rumpling his ears.

" I have something of Lord Hareby's here," he explained, producing a sock that we had discovered lying by the side of the path. " Let us go to where we lost the trail, and introduce Bosker to the scent."

On sniffing the sock, and being led to the point on the driveway where the visible tracks ceased, the hound struck out without hesitation in a path that led towards the rear of the Hall. " Good lad, Bosker," Hanshaw encouraged him. " Go it, boy." We followed the dog, Holmes gripping the leash, until we came to a low circular wall behind the kitchens. The hound put his front paws on the lip of the well, for so it appeared to be, and howled dismally.

Realisation struck me. " This is the well that is used for the Ritual of the Mace ? "

Hanshaw nodded silently. His face was grim.

" We must assume the worst," said Holmes, bluntly. " Hanshaw, how deep is this well ? "

" Some fifty feet or so to the water, sir."

" There is no ladder on the estate long enough to reach down ? "

" No, sir. In any event, the water is bottomless, they say. I am not sure that any ladder on this earth could find the bottom of the well. I will return Bosker to the kennels, and return with one of the stable-lads and a stout rope."

" Very good, Hanshaw. A man of whom Lord Darlington should be proud," remarked Holmes as the coachman departed. " He has his wits about him and can think for himself. The Metropolitan Police could use him and more like him."

" Assuming that we discover Lord Hareby there," I said, motioning to the well, " in your opinion, what was the reason for his action ? "

" Obviously the same cause that made him run naked through the fields. At present we have no facts on which to build theories, and I do not propose doing so at this time."

We waited in silence, not daring to speak in the presence of whatever lay below us in the well. Eventually, Hanshaw returned, two coils of stout rope looped over one shoulder, and followed by a young red-haired lad I judged to be about eighteen years of age, carrying a horse-blanket.

" Robbins here will go down the well," announced Hanshaw.

" Has he told you what you may discover down there ? " asked Holmes solicitously. " You are prepared for that ? "

The boy nodded. " Can't say as I'm looking forward to it, sir, but it's a job that's got to be done."

" Excellent. I would recommend that you remove as many

of your garments as will retain your decency, in order to provide the greatest freedom of movement."

The boy looked a little blank.

" Strip down so you can move about down there," Hanshaw amplified. " You'll probably get yourself wet, and you're going to need some dry clothes when you come up."

" Thank you," smiled Holmes. He took one of the ropes, and deftly fashioned some kind of harness from it, using complex knots. " There, that should do the trick," he exclaimed at length. " I learned this arrangement from an old sailor, so have no fear." He looped the harness around the boy's shoulders and under his arms. " Are you ready? "

Robbins nodded mutely, his face pale. " Let us all take the other end," suggested Holmes.

Slowly we lowered the stable-lad down the well. As Hanshaw had told us, the depth was considerable and by my estimation we had paid out about fifty feet of rope before the voice from below called to us to stop. While still gripping the rope tightly, we moved closer to the mouth of the well to hear what Robbins had to say to us.

" I think this is him," floated up to us from the depths, spoken in a tone that signified disgust and repulsion. " I'm not going to be able to bring him up, though."

" I will send another rope down to you," called down Holmes. " Tie it around his waist. We will pull you up first, and then pull him up. Can you manage to do that? "

" I'll do my best, sir." The voice was wavering, but there was some confidence in it.

Hanshaw bent over the well and called down encouragement. " That's right, lad. Do your best. You can't do any more than that. Give it your best shot. The rope's coming down now." He carefully lowered one end of the rope down the well, giving and receiving instructions to Robbins, until we received the report that the rope was made fast. "We'll pull you up now, lad," called down Hanshaw. "Help yourself up, and mind your knees and elbows." We pulled together on the rope and shortly brought Robbins, dripping and shivering, to the surface. "Here you are," Hanshaw said to him, wrapping the blanket around the boy's shaking shoulders.

Holmes pulled his hip-flask from his pocket and offered it to Robbins.

"Should I?" the stable-lad asked Hanshaw, who nodded.

"Go on. It will do you good and warm you up. I won't tell your Ma. He's chapel," he explained to Holmes and myself as Robbins accepted the flask and took a cautious sip. After he had patted the coughing boy on the back and returned the flask to Holmes, he sighed. "We're going to have to bring him up," he commented.

"True enough," agreed Holmes, and we gingerly hauled on the second rope, taking care as the hideous burden swayed and bumped against the sides of the well.

"That's him," said Hanshaw, as the dripping naked corpse cleared the rim of the wall. "Turn your back and get dressed now, Robbins. You don't want to see him, and we need the blanket, anyway."

The dead man's face was contorted in agony, and I bent over the body to examine it as Holmes and Hanshaw laid it gently on the blanket.

"He was in pain, obviously," I remarked. "There is a curious flush to the skin that I would not have expected, and I cannot immediately account for it." I pulled up one of the eyelids and peered at the dead man's eyes. "The eyes are turned up," I remarked. "I am unsure of the reason for that also."

"Let us wrap him in the blanket and take him inside. Hanshaw, from what I can see, you are close to Lord Darlington. Do you feel you can tell him what has happened?"

"Like Robbins here said just now, sir, all I can tell you is that I'll do my best. Come on now, lad," he said to Robbins. " He's all wrapped up now and you can look, if you really want to."

" Good man. And maybe I shall take care of the task of informing Lady Hareby."

" I'd be grateful if you'd do that, sir. It's going to be bad enough telling his Lordship about what's happened without me having to face her as well."

" Very good. Let us take him together through the back entrance to the Hall."

Slowly, the four of us carried our blanket-shrouded burden to the kitchen entrance, and from there up the back stairs to the bed-room where Lord Hareby had spent his last night.

" Thank you, gentlemen," said Holmes.

" No more than our duty, sir, but a sad one. I am glad you found him so quickly, though. Now I will find his Lordship and break the sad news to him."

Holmes and I were left alone in the room, and I gently unwrapped the body from the horse-blanket.

" I must leave you, and inform Lady Hareby," Holmes said to me. " I would like you to make an examination of the body as thoroughly as you can under the circumstances before anyone else arrives in this room."

" Is there anything in particular you want me to look for ? " I asked him as he stepped out of the door.

" The mouth and tongue," he replied.

I drew a sheet over the body up to the chin, noting the red inflamed skin as I did so. From my experience, such an inflammation would be accompanied by a burning itching sensation, which would explain why he had thrown off his clothes in the way he had.

Opening the mouth, I was struck by the colour of the tongue, which was a livid purple, as was the roof of the mouth.

I heard footsteps outside the door, and hurriedly closed

the mouth and arranged the limbs in a seemly posture before throwing the sheet over the whole body. Unfortunately, the face still bore the marks of agony, for which I was unable to provide any remedy.

As I finished, the door opened, and the Earl walked in, supporting himself on a stick, his face racked with pain.

"Doctor," he addressed me. "Hanshaw has just informed me of what has occurred. Is that him?" gesturing to the sheet-draped figure.

"It is, sir."

"May I see him?"

"I warn you, sir, that he is probably not as you wish to remember him."

"Never mind. He is—was my son," he corrected himself. "Draw back the sheet," he ordered me.

I did so, exposing the face, into which the Earl stared for a full two minutes in silence, at the end of which he nodded to me to replace the sheet. "I see all now," he said. "It is that she-devil who drove him to this."

I took his meaning instantly, and at that moment, Holmes re-entered the room, preceded by Lady Hareby. The old man glared at his daughter-in-law with a face of fury, and actually shook his stick at her.

"I will see you hanged for this," he spat out at her as he left the room.

The door banged shut on his exit, and Lady Hareby regarded Holmes and myself with an air of injured innocence. "The grief has turned his brain," she said lightly. "How he thinks that I could ever be found responsible for Edgar's death ... It is the fancy of a foolish old man. I have been with my child all morning, and the nurse will bear witness to that fact. That is Edgar?" she asked, gesturing towards the bed.

"Yes, it is." I made as if to draw down the sheet again, but she held up a hand to stop me.

"No, do not. I have no wish to look upon his face. Thank you both for your part in this."

"Our part in this business is not yet complete," answered Holmes.

"What do you mean by that?"

"I would have thought the meaning of my words was perfectly clear to you, Lady Hareby," he replied calmly.

"Mr. Holmes! Are you insinuating—?"

"I am insinuating nothing. If you choose to draw any conclusions at all from my words, that is entirely your own affair."

"It seems I should not underestimate you, then?"

"Many have done so in the past. It was so much the worse for them," he replied.

"I will see you gentlemen this afternoon at the Ritual of the Mace, I take it?" she asked with an air of innocence.

"Why, will it still take place?" I asked in astonishment.

"Of course, my dear Doctor" she smiled. "Life must go on, even after such a tragic experience as this."

With those words, she swept out of the room. I let out a long breath.

"A dangerous woman, I think, Watson. She impresses me more every time I have the misfortune to come into range. Well, what did you discover?"

I informed him of what I had seen inside the mouth of the dead man, and he nodded. "I was expecting something of the sort. Poison, quite obviously, but of a kind I am unable to identify at this remove from my works of reference. I am reluctant to travel to London simply to read a few words, particularly when Lord Darlington's life also hangs by a thread."

"Lord Darlington!" I ejaculated. "Granted that he suffers from gout, and that his health seems to be precarious, but what are you implying?"

"He is now," pointed out Holmes, "the only life that now stands between Lady Hareby and her child, and this estate."

" You cannot mean— ? "

" I can and I do, and I see it as my duty to protect him from that woman in whatever way it takes."

There was a sudden knock on the door, and the elderly doctor I had met on my last visit appeared in the door, his face a mask of worry.

" I was told you were here, Doctor," he said to me. " I have been told the news. Shocking, shocking." He swayed a little, and hiccoughed gently. " Have you signed the death certificate? What did you put as the cause of death, eh? Drowning? "

" Indeed, I have done no such thing," I replied stiffly. I have been unable to determine a cause of death, and I am going to recommend that an autopsy be performed."

" Should have thought it was simple enough," replied Brendell. " Man goes outside for the first time in weeks, feels weak and dizzy, sits down on the edge of the well and falls in. Simple. Accidental death."

" Hardly that," replied Holmes, who, to my astonishment and that of the inebriated doctor, seized the latter firmly by the shoulders, spun him around, and propelled him out of the door.

" Well, bless my soul," he exclaimed as he left the room. " I never expected to receive such treatment."

" Be that as it may," muttered Holmes, chiefly to himself, " you have received it and may consider yourself lucky that it was not accompanied by a hearty kick. Now," he addressed himself to me, " we must look around this room for any signs of foul play in the form of poison having been administered. It may, of course, have been administered in his breakfast, or it may have been a slow-acting poison administered the previous night, but my guess is that he himself ingested it here unknowingly. The alternatives, while not impossible, would seem less likely."

" But what here could he have put in his mouth ? "

" Come now. There are many possibilities here. The water he drank upon rising, or the water he used to rinse his mouth after cleaning his teeth. Come to that, we might suspect his very tooth-powder, or the medicines he was taking for his various conditions."

" That old fraud Brendell informed me that most of the medicines he prescribed were in fact not medicines at all, but were no more than alcohol and water. Anything added to them would almost certainly be instantly detectable." Nonetheless, I went over to the tray on the night-table and examined the bottles there. One of the bottles caught my eye. " Holmes," I called to him. " Do you remember last month that I mentioned that a bottle of patent medicine had disappeared from the tray ? "

" Of course."

" It has returned."

" Presumably you are looking at a replacement bottle of the same type."

" No," I insisted. " This is the identical bottle. I remember a particular tear with a distinctive pattern in the top right corner of the label. This is the same bottle that I saw earlier, and I would take my oath on that in court."

" Does it contain any of the tonic ? " asked Holmes.

I picked up the bottle and examined it. " About one-third full, I would say."

" And it is a pick-me-up to induce vitality ? Such as a recent invalid might use to dose himself before a spell of unaccustomed exercise ? "

" I begin to see your meaning." I opened the bottle, and was about to smell the liquid when Holmes stopped me.

" I do not want you to expose yourself to such a risk," he admonished me. " At present we have no knowledge of what the poison is, or how it works. The mere inhalation of the vapour may be sufficient to produce harmful effects."

"You are assuming that this is the medium in which the poison was administered, then?"

"I am certain of it. Observe the tray. There is a thin film of dust covering its surface, as there is of many of the bottles. Now," and he lifted one of the bottles in question, "this bottle has left a circle beneath it, clean and free of dust."

"So I see."

"Whereas by contrast this tonic bottle not only is free of dust itself, but the portion of the tray on which it stood is covered with dust. The inference is clear. This bottle was placed on the tray very recently—perhaps even last night."

"With the expectation that the sick man would wish to use it in the morning?"

"Exactly. We were told that Lord Hareby went out for a constitutional yesterday. Obviously his condition was improving. But maybe he complained of fatigue following his exercise, and expressed a wish for his favourite nostrum to be provided again for his use. What better vehicle for the poison?"

"It would take a diabolical mind, Holmes, to be capable of such a thing."

"And do you believe there is no such mind in this house at the moment?" he chided me. "We know full well there is such a one. And she is close at hand. Come, there is no time to lose." He scooped up the bottle of tonic and placed it carefully in an inside pocket of his coat. "We will not lose the evidence again. This will be analysed on our return to London."

We made our way along the oak-panelled passageway, when we were stopped by the sound of a baby's crying, seemingly coming from a room in front of us. I admit that I froze in some fear, having heard Bouverie's tales of the invisible and untraceable baby, but Holmes strode on ahead to the source of the sound, and flung open a door, to reveal a young baby rocked in the arms of a young woman, obviously its nurse, and who was murmuring words of comfort in its ear to stop its crying.

"My apologies," said Holmes to the nurse, closing the door and turning to me. "Nothing strange there, you will admit?"

"It would appear not. But remember we were informed that the crying occurred even when the baby was observed to be sleeping."

"I had not forgotten that," he answered me, somewhat testily. "Where is Lady Hareby? We were told she was mostly to be found with her child. I begin to be concerned."

We continued to walk down the passage, Holmes seemingly lost in thought, when he suddenly seized my arm and pulled me to one side. "Hide yourself. Do not let yourself be seen," he hissed in my ear. He and I ducked into the closest doorway. "Look!" He pointed down the passage. Lady Hareby was now in the passageway, walking away from us.

"Where did she come from?" I whispered in Holmes' ear. "There are no doors that I can see between us and her, from which she might have emerged."

"Precisely," he agreed. "Let us wait until she has descended the stairs at the end of the passage, and we will investigate."

In a matter of a minute or less, Lady Hareby had left the passage and was now, it might be assumed, safely downstairs. Holmes and I left our place of concealment and made our way towards where we had seen her. As I had noted, there were no doors visible, and it was impossible for us to judge from where she had appeared.

"I refuse to accept the impossible," declared Holmes. "It is outside the laws of science as we understand them for a human being to appear suddenly from nowhere."

"I agree with you, but I see no alternative."

By way of answer, Holmes moved to the head of the stairs

at the end of the passage, turned abruptly, and strode the full length of the passageway to the other end, before returning.

" And now we go upstairs to the servants' quarters."

" Should we not ask permission ? "

" A man's life may be at stake," he retorted, and sprang up the stairs leading to the servants' rooms, two at a time. Once there, he repeated the process that he had previously undertaken on the floor below, pacing the length of the corridor. " It fits, Watson, it all fits," was his only comment, and I could get no more out of him.

We were just about to make our way down the stairs, when Holmes stopped and cocked his head. " Do you not hear it ? " he asked. I listened carefully, and could distinguish the wail of an infant in distress.

" That is not the sound of the baby downstairs. It would appear to be coming from behind that wall."

" That is where I also would locate it," replied Holmes. " Come." We made our way downstairs to the ground floor. " The library," he commanded, and we made our way to that room, where we saw the Earl, huddled in an armchair, wrapped in his own thoughts, which from the expression on his face, were ones of misery.

" Have you any good news for me ? " he asked Holmes. " Quite frankly, I do not feel that I wish to live any longer. My hopes have been dashed and my spirit is broken."

" But you will perform the Ritual of the Mace this afternoon as planned ? " Holmes asked.

" I must, if it is the last act I perform on this earth," replied Lord Darlington. He lifted his face, and I beheld an air of ravaged nobility that transcended his obvious despair.

" Either Watson or I will be by your side until that time," said Holmes. " Although I have no good news on which you can rely absolutely, I feel that by the end of the day, we will have answers to some of the questions that have troubled you for many months."

"I pray to God you are right," replied the old man fervently.

"Sherlock Holmes never makes mistakes," I assured him.

"Let us not say 'never'," smiled Holmes. "But in this instance, I feel it is hardly possible for me to have made a mistake." He turned to me. "I will give orders for Lord Darlington's luncheon to be served in here, along with yours. I would request you, though I realise it is an imposition, to taste a little of each part of each dish served to Lord Darlington. You mentioned, sir," turning to him, "that your palate was no longer keen, and I would like Watson to use his younger and fresher senses to act as a detector in the event of any strong taste being present in your food."

"You expect poison?" asked the old man incredulously.

"I do not say that I expect it, but it is a possibility," replied Holmes. "Watson, pray take care."

"May I ask where you are going?" I asked him.

"I must make preparations for this afternoon," he replied. "I wish to make the Ritual as complete as possible." So saying, he left us, leaving the Earl and I shaking our heads.

As you may well imagine, the responsibility with which Holmes had entrusted me weighed heavily on my mind. Even assuming that there was an attempt made to poison Lord Darlington, neither Holmes nor myself had any idea of the type of poison or the dose needed to produce results, let alone any antidote. Nonetheless, I determined to do my duty.

Luncheon arrived on a tray, and I tasted the clear soup that began the meal. There was nothing untoward about it, and I informed Lord Darlington that in my opinion, it was safe to partake. Next came a sirloin of beef, with boiled potatoes and carrots. Again, after a sampling of the different parts of the meal, I gave my approval. Lord Darlington was about to convey the first forkful of food to his mouth, when I stayed his hand.

"I am sorry," I said to him, "but I omitted to taste the horseradish sauce you are eating with the beef."

"Oh, really, Watson," he protested.

"Even so, I gave my word to Holmes." I took a little of the horseradish in my mouth. It was, as I had expected, hot, but there was a bitter underlying taste to it that I had never before discerned in horseradish. "I really do not recommend that you eat any of that horseradish," I told him.

"Very well," he grumbled, "though at my age it is almost the only thing that has any savour to it," and he pointedly ignored the relish for the rest of the meal.

For myself, I felt a hot flush and an uncomfortable itching sensation developing, and though it was uncomfortable to a high degree, it was by no means intolerable. Lord Darlington, however, commented on my flushed state, which I now began to realise was a less serious version of the symptoms that had afflicted poor Lord Hareby. Certainly, even the minute dose of the poison that I had received from my taste of the horseradish was sufficient to cause extreme discomfort. I could only imagine the agony which Lord Hareby had suffered as the result of a larger dose, taken while he was in a weaker state.

Nonetheless, I continued to taste everything set before us, finding nothing untoward in the rhubarb and custard. We had just finished our meal when Holmes re-entered, rubbing his hands together with an air of satisfaction.

"You have eaten well, I trust?" he asked, and then noticed my face. "You are in pain, Watson?" he asked with an air of genuine concern. "Shall I call a doctor—not Dr. Brendell, naturally?"

I reassured him that though I was experiencing some discomfort, I did not consider myself to be in any danger, and indeed, the burning and itching was lessening as I spoke.

"Where was it?" asked Holmes. On my informing him that the horseradish almost certainly contained the poison, he exclaimed, somewhat to the surprise of Lord Darlington, and to my amusement, "Naturally. That is where I would have placed it myself, had I had charge of the operation. Do not worry, sir," he reassured the peer. "You should understand that the small successes I have enjoyed in the apprehension of criminals are at least in part due to the ability to put myself in the wrongdoers' place, and thereby anticipate their next moves." Lord Darlington appeared to be a little relieved at this. "And now, I believe, to the Ritual. I noticed the worthy Hanshaw making the arrangements by the well, and Bouverie appeared to be preparing Lady Hareby and her son to go outside."

"Very well," replied Lord Darlington, rising slowly to his feet.

"Have you the Mace?" asked Holmes.

"It is here," replied the other, picking up a cloth-wrapped bundle that lay beside him on a side-table.

Chapter XII

Rebecca Johnson

I T was a sombre procession that made its way to the fatal well. I could not repress a shudder when I beheld it, and remembered what ghastly object we had dragged from its depths. The Earl faltered in his steps at the sight of the well, even though he had not been present, and of us three, only Holmes appeared to be unmoved.

A group was standing by the well ; Lady Hareby to one side of the other two: Bouverie, and the woman whom Holmes and I had seen earlier, presumably the nurse of the baby, as she was holding a white-wrapped bundle in her arms.

A group of servants stood a little way off. I could see Hanshaw, but failed to observe the young boy Robbins who had retrieved the body of Lord Hareby.

The Earl approached the well, leaning heavily on his stick, and unwrapped the Mace. With an effort, he extracted the last coin from the head of the ancient gnarled root, and held it aloft.

" Listen well, ye of Hareby Hall," he intoned, as if reciting some ancient text. " This is the last of the silver pennies that were bequeathed to my ancestor by Mad Maggie eleven generations before. When this coin is lost in the depths of the well, as my poor son has already been lost … " Here his voice faltered, and there was a catch in his throat. " My poor son, as you know, has gone before," he continued, " and when this coin falls to the bottom of the well, his son, George, Lord Wittingford, takes his place, becomes the new rightful heir to Hareby and takes on his father's title. Then, when I leave this earth, he takes mine. The last of his line. God save us all." With a sob, he drew back his arm as if to throw the blackened silver disc, but was halted in his action by a sudden cry from one of the servants.

" Fire ! The Hall is on fire ! " he shouted, pointing upward to a window.

Sure enough, dark smoke billowed forth from the window, and a voice could be heard shouting from within.

There was a horrified silence as the assembly took in the sight, suddenly broken by a scream from Lady Hareby.

" My baby ! " she shrieked, and, picking up her skirts, fairly ran in the direction of the Hall.

" But her baby is here," I said to Holmes, puzzled by this action, and pointing to the infant in the nurse's arms.

" I fancy not," replied Holmes, smiling.

" Then what or who is that … ? "

" We will, I fancy, hear the truth from the lips of Lady Hareby, even though it may take some time to discover it."

" But what about the fire ? " exclaimed Lord Darlington, his face twitching in agitation. " Quick, everybody must work to extinguish it ! Water ! Buckets ! " he shouted to the assembled servants.

Holmes held up his hand. " There is no need," he said calmly. " Look," pointing up at the window which had been the source of the billowing smoke, and from which only a few faint wisps now emerged.

" Well, that is certainly providential," remarked Lord Darlington. " Hanshaw, go up there and ensure that all is safe, if you would."

For some reason that I could not fully comprehend, Hanshaw darted a curious look towards Holmes, who gave an almost imperceptible nod before the coachman started for the Hall.

" Holmes," I whispered to him, " I believe you know more about this business than you are admitting at present."

" I would prefer not to speak of it now," he replied. " My main concern is with Lady Hareby."

" Where is she ? "

" That is what we must discover now. Come." He set off at a brisk pace following the path that had just been taken by Hanshaw, and I followed.

We climbed the stairs to the passage where we had earlier seen Lady Hareby miraculously appear. To my surprise, one of the oak panels lining the wall had swung open, revealing a narrow stone staircase.

"In the days of the Reformation or King James, this would have been a priest's hole, no doubt," remarked Holmes. "Hidden from prying eyes, and leading to a secret hiding place where Romish priests could escape their persecutors."

"And now?" I could not help but ask.

"It has served a very different purpose, but I fear we are too late."

As he spoke, I heard the noise of footsteps descending and coming towards us. The coachman, Hanshaw, came into view, his arms raised above his head and a look of fear on his face. The terror was explained when close behind him, a white bundle in one arm, and a small pistol in the other hand, Lady Hareby came into view.

"Let us pass, gentlemen," she said to Holmes in a cold tone. "Hanshaw here will be driving me to the station, from where I will catch a train to London. You may choose to follow me, but I doubt that you will find me."

Holmes shrugged. "I fear you have a poor opinion of my abilities," he replied. "Are you not fearful for your daughter's safety, however?" gesturing to the white bundle.

Lady Hareby regarded him with something like wonder in her eyes. "Maybe I did underestimate you once, Mr. Holmes. I have no intention of repeating the mistake, though."

"We must stop her!" I cried, starting forward, but Holmes restrained me. "More haste, less speed. There will be time enough to catch up with the whole story in the future. Besides," he added pleasantly, "neither you nor I have any wish to place Hanshaw in any jeopardy."

"That's right, sir," replied Hanshaw, smiling despite himself.

"Oh, you think you are so clever, Mr. Holmes," exclaimed

Lady Hareby bitterly. " In the past ten minutes you may well have robbed me of thousands of pounds and thwarted the plans of several years. Believe me, you are not so clever as you may believe yourself, and I will have my revenge." She swept out, driving Hanshaw before her at the point of her pistol.

" Why did you not stop her ? " I asked when she was out of sight.

" There is little need at present. I hope that by allowing her to reach London, she will lead us to the other players in the game."

" And what of the child she was carrying? You said it was her daughter ? " Holmes nodded. " Who or what is that child outside that we believed was her son ? "

" That is what we will find out. Let us go upstairs."

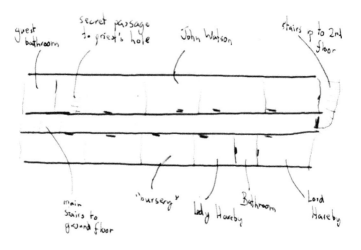

(I attach the above sketch of the first floor as a guide to show the relative positions of the rooms on the floor from which we ascended)

We mounted the narrow twisting stone staircase to the floor above, where we found ourselves in a small room, lit only by the sunlight filtering through a small skylight in the roof. A young woman sat by an empty crib, weeping.

"Who are you?" asked Holmes, not unkindly. "Are you the boy's mother?"

She shook her head. "No, sir. I don't know what boy you're talking about. I was hired by the lady when I was down in London to come here and take care of the little girl, and wet-nurse her, and she's taken her away now, just as I was getting fond of the poor little dear."

"I am sorry to hear that," said Holmes. "Tell me, what food have you been eating?" His eyes were on a tray by the chair.

"The lady brought me my meals. Not too many of them and there wasn't a lot to them, to be sure."

"How long have you been here?" Holmes asked.

"Two weeks, I suppose. I have lost count of the days up here."

"You had better come downstairs," Holmes told her, extending his hand. "Come."

The three of us made our way downstairs where the Earl and Bouverie awaited us.

"Bless me," exclaimed the old man. "Who is this, and what was she doing in the priest's hole?"

The young woman bobbed a curtsey. "Please, sir, my name is Mary Windsor, and I came to this house to look after the little girl."

The Earl looked astounded, as well he might, and Holmes placed a kindly hand on his shoulder. "Bouverie, Miss Windsor here will be pleased, I am sure, to inform you about the source of the wailing and crying that has been disturbing the household. I would suggest that you take care of Miss Windsor and ensure she is comfortable. I believe the last two weeks have been somewhat trying for her, though she has had the good manners not to mention this."

"Thank you, sir," replied the girl. "You are perfectly correct."

"And, sir, now that your daughter-in-law is on her way to London—" The Earl started at this, and Holmes gestured through the window at the vista beyond. The trap was visible in the act of leaving the driveway. "—I will explain all if you come downstairs. But first let me send some instructions." He ripped a page from his notebook and scrawled a few lines, giving it to Bouverie, together with a sovereign and instructions that his message be taken by one of the outdoor servants to the village post office and dispatched by telegram to London as soon as possible.

Once seated in the library, Holmes addressed Lord Darlington and myself.

"You were correct in your suspicions and doubts regarding Lady Hareby. I am convinced that she was directly responsible for your son's illness of the heart that took him to hospital, and that she also encompassed his death."

The old man sat with his head in his hands. "I had always believed it to be an imprudent match," he explained. "But he was not to be persuaded. If only his dear mother had lived, he might have changed his mind. But … "

"Love will have its way," replied Holmes. "Or rather, in this case, perhaps the word 'infatuation' might be more appropriate.

"It is clear that she married your son, with the intention of gaining control of the estate after your death. I think that much is obvious from her actions and from her behaviour towards her husband and towards you. Earlier, she had almost killed Lord Hareby by preying on his superstitious fears. The books provided for his entertainment in his bed-room were almost certainly provided by her, in order to heighten his fancies, and to weaken his will.

"The Mace, as you have almost certainly deduced for

yourself, sir, was abstracted by her from the cabinet here in the library, and was treated in such a way as to make it a frightening object when beheld at the dead of night, especially by a man in his frail condition. I have no doubt that it was these manipulations that were responsible for his sudden illness that morning. Whence the idea originated, and from whom she obtained the luminous compound to make it shine in the dark, I am confident that I shall shortly discover.

" Naturally, she is unable to inherit the estate in her own right, according to the terms of entailment. The full control of the estate and its revenues could only be attained through her child, or more specifically, her son. For her, this was a wager – that the child she was carrying was male. As I remarked to Watson earlier, it would be staking all on the toss of a coin. If the child proved to be female, then all would be lost. Her husband was almost certainly incapable of providing her with another child. She therefore, to continue my analogy, therefore had to provide herself with a double-headed coin. She made enquiries down in London with the aim of procuring a new-born baby boy, again from sources as yet unknown to me, and the aim was to pass it off as her own. Tell me, sir, who was present at the birth of her child ? "

" Not I, naturally. Nor my son. Dr. Brendell was the physician, but now I come to recall, he was late in arriving, and he was not actually present at the birth. Only the village midwife was in attendance."

" I will need to speak to her soon. Please send one of your people down to the village to bring her here."

The Earl rang and gave the order for the midwife to be brought to the Hall as soon as possible.

" Once she had a child whom she could present as the next heir, the way was clear for her to eliminate her husband entirely. It is almost certain that it was she who dosed his tonic with a deadly poison, the exact composition of which is still a mystery to me, which had the effect of irritating the skin and causing a temporary loss of sanity. Dr. Watson here was subjected to a very minor dose of this drug which had been introduced into the horseradish at luncheon today. Once again, Watson, I owe you my apologies for subjecting you to this."

"And I owe you my thanks," added the peer to me. "Almost certainly I would have succumbed had not been due to your courage, and the diligence of Mr. Holmes."

I was agog to ask Holmes how he had come to the conclusion that he had reached regarding the existence of the priest's hole, as well as the way in which he had managed the fire (for there was not the faintest doubt in my mind that he was the genius behind that incident), but I knew it was fruitless to quiz him on these matters unless he chose to speak of them.

"I wonder what will become of Mad Maggie's curse now," said the Earl, reflectively, a wry smile on his lips. "Is the curse now broken, as the coin was not thrown into the well, and we have no heir?"

"That is a question whose answer falls outside my sphere," replied Holmes sternly. "I deal in facts and physical evidence. You must seek elsewhere for the answer to that question."

We sat together in silence for a few minutes, broken at length by Bouverie's entrance and his announcement of the arrival of the village midwife.

"Show her in, then," the Earl told him. A minute later, an ancient crone hobbled into the room, and gazed at Holmes and me suspiciously.

"A good afternoon to your Lordship," she croaked. "And who may these two be?"

"These are two gentlemen from London who want to ask you a few questions, Rebecca," answered the Earl. "Won't you sit down?" indicating a chair.

"I will, thanking you, sir," replied the old woman, continuing to glare at us. "So you two gentlemen have come all the way from London to ask me some questions?"

" That is correct," replied Holmes.

" I must warn you gentlemen that my memory is not what it once was. It would be a waste of time for you to ask me about things that happened long ago."

" This is about something that happened only two weeks ago. I am sure your memory is not that poor."

She frowned in response. " Are you wanting me to talk about her Ladyship ? " she answered. " Because if you are, I can tell you now that you are wasting your time." She set her hands on her knees and sat in her chair solidly.

" That is a pity," said Holmes, rising, and making as if to leave the room.

" Where are you going ? " she asked him.

" You told me that I was wasting my time," replied Holmes coolly. " I see no point in my continuing this conversation. Maybe you would prefer to speak to me from a police cell."

" Why would I be in a police cell ? " she asked, obviously troubled by this prospect.

" Because you are withholding evidence necessary for the solving of a crime," he answered. " Lord Darlington, I take it you have no objection to my sending one of your servants to fetch the police."

" You can't be doing that ! " exclaimed the old woman. " I've done nothing I shouldn't have done."

" How much did she pay you ?   Five shillings ? " asked Holmes.

" Five shillings ? I have my standards, thanking you kindly, Mr. Busybody," replied the old woman, making a motion as if to spit on the floor, but then appearing to remember where she was, and thinking better of it. " It was ten guineas—not pounds, mark you, but guineas." She suddenly realised what she had admitted, and clapped a hand to her mouth.

" Somewhat in excess of your usual fee as a midwife, I would expect ? " replied Holmes. " And how did you earn all this extra money ? "

" It was a girl," she muttered. " I'd told her it would be, be-cause I'd swung her wedding ring over her belly a month be-fore. It swung round and round in a circle like it does when it's going to be a girl. If it's a boy, it just goes back and forward."

" Indeed," said Holmes, hiding his obvious amusement at this piece of rustic superstition. " I live and learn. So what was Lady Hareby's reaction when you told her?"

" She told me it had to be a boy, and she was going to make sure that it was a boy. I don't know what she did in London when she went down there, but next I know was that just about her time, there was a knock on my door, and there was a man standing there with this little baby in his arms.

" 'Hello,' says he, 'and you are Rebecca Johnson?'

" 'I am,' I says back to him, 'and who are you, and who's that little one you've got there?'

" 'Never you mind who I am," he says, 'but this here is Lady Hareby's new-born son.'

" 'He hasn't been born yet,' says I, and I look a bit closer at the baby. 'In any event, that's no new-born,' I tells him. 'That baby's two weeks old at least.'

" 'There's few at the Hall who'll know the difference,' he says. 'And those who do won't say anything.'

" By now I had some idea of what was going on. 'When my Ladyship's time comes,' I says to him, 'you want me to change the baby if it's a girl so that she has a new baby boy to show the world.'

" 'She said you were a quick one.'

" 'And what happens to the poor little girl?' I asked. I'm soft-hearted, like, and I didn't want to think of anything hap-pening to a new baby. I mean to say, I had no idea what was going to happen to the new little one.

" 'There'll be someone who will take care of her. She'll be well looked after.' Well, that put my mind at rest a bit, I can tell you. I mean, it's one thing to change one baby for another, but there was no way I was going to be involved in anything rough."

"Your sentiments do you credit," observed Holmes, acidly.

Oblivious of the sarcasm in his voice, the old woman continued. "'What if it's a boy?' I asks him.

"'You said it was going to be a girl,' he says.

"'I did, but the pendulum's sometimes wrong,' I had to tell him. I'm telling you gentlemen that it doesn't always work. Sometimes you get the wrong feeling and it starts to rock back and forward and you don't know what's going on, and—"

"And then what happened?" Holmes was obviously making an effort to keep the exasperation out of his voice.

"Well, he gave me five guineas, 'to be getting on with' he said, and told me that there would be another five after the birth and the change. Well, it was a close thing him coming the day he did, because it was the very next morning that her Ladyship's waters broke and I was called in. Doctor Brendell had been drinking the night before, I guess, and couldn't be there in time, so I was the only one they could find. I went along with the little boy all wrapped up and did what I had to do. And just as I had told her, it was a lovely little baby girl. I gave the little thing to one of the new maids who'd just started and she carried her out of the room to somewhere else. But before she did, she gave me the five extra guineas that I'd been promised.

"Then I dressed up the little boy and made it look as though he was the new-born, and then Dr. Brendell came in. And a waste of time it was him coming in. It was all over by then."

"Thank you," said Holmes. "That is most helpful. One more thing. Can you describe the man who brought the baby boy?"

She frowned. "Well, he was about the height of that

gentleman there or a bit less," pointing to me. "Youngish, about twenty-five, I'd say. Not a day over thirty, anyway. A bit stout and dark-looking. No beard or moustache to him. In fact, he looked a bit of a baby face to me. Spoke like a toff, but looked more like a gypsy with those ears of his."

"What about his ears?" asked Holmes, leaning forward intently.

"Well, they had holes in them like the gypsies do when they want to put earrings in them."

"Aha," Holmes said quietly. "That is extremely interesting."

"And there's one more odd thing about him, sir," she went on. "He had this strange white sort of splash mark here," pointing to her own forehead.

It suddenly occurred to me that I myself had encountered this man some time before while walking in the Park, and I was about to remark on the circumstance, but Holmes spoke.

"Had he, indeed? That is most gratifying to hear. I think, sir," turning to the Earl, "that since Mrs. Johnson was paid ten guineas to keep the secret, at least an equal sum could be provided for her since she has now revealed it."

"What? Oh, yes, I suppose so. I will make the arrangements."

"Why, thank you, sirs," replied the old crone, smiling almost for the first time since she had entered the room. "Thank you," she repeated, rising slowly to her feet, and being shown to the door by the Earl.

"We must to London, Watson," Holmes addressed me. "As soon as the worthy Hanshaw returns from his little adventure, I am afraid we must trouble him or one of his fellows to convey Watson and myself to the station."

"You believe him to be safe?" Lord Darlington asked anxiously.

"Of course. Her threat to shoot Hanshaw was, of course,

merely a bluff. She could not drive herself to the station, so shooting him would defeat her purposes. In addition, any act of violence against him here would simply leave her as a proven criminal surrounded by witnesses."

"You relieve my mind," replied the Earl.

S the express train carried us back to London, I could not refrain from asking Holmes to whom he had addressed the telegram he had caused to be sent from Hareby, and what the contents of it had been.

"I addressed it to Inspector Athelney Jones," he replied. "He is not possessed of a multitude of redeeming features as a detective, but as a watchdog he has few equals within the Force. His task is to watch for Lady Hareby and to mark where she takes herself on alighting from the train."

"Not to arrest her?" I asked.

"At present, I do not have enough evidence to secure a conviction. Jones would be a fool to proceed any further with the case at this stage of the proceedings. Especially when you take into account the fact that she is a young mother, with a new-born infant, she would have to commit murder or worse under the very eyes of the jury in order for her to be convicted. I require much more in the way of hard facts before Jones can take such a step."

"But the bottle of tonic, the Mace that you discovered in the creeper outside the house!" I protested. "I am a witness to those things."

"Watson," he remonstrated. "You are, as I have remarked before, the epitome of true English reliability and solidity. They are estimable qualities, and I admire your possession of them. In the vast majority of cases, your testimony would carry absolute conviction to twelve good men and true. However, when the defendant is one such as Lady Hareby, a young woman of considerable personal attractiveness, recently widowed, and the mother of an adorable young baby—"

" How do you know it is adorable ? " I broke in. " You have not even seen its face."

" All young babies are adorable to certain classes of person, including jurors," he replied sourly. " As I was saying, your testimony would carry no weight with a jury against a witness such as Lady Hareby."

" What exactly are you seeking to discover in London ? "

" I wish to know the full story of the infant that she was passing off as the heir to the Hareby estate. This is not something that she could have accomplished on her own, and I therefore believe that she was aided by person or persons who are outside the law. Whether she realises it or not, she has placed herself in their power. I am in hopes that she will lead me to the spider at the centre of the web. For several years it has been obvious to me that there is a central mind controlling almost all the major, and many of the minor criminal actions committed in London. I can see his traces in many of his subordinates' actions and methods, but I am still unaware of his identity. I promise you that if I were able to lay hold of him, London would become a peaceful paradise compared to what it is now."

" And you, my dear Holmes, would find yourself with nothing to occupy you," I laughed.

" True. I do not see myself stooping to divorce cases or similar sordid matters. On the other hand, do you not think that I could justly congratulate myself on such a result ? "

" First, as the cookery book so rightly advises, you must catch your hare, however."

" As so often, Watson, you are perfectly correct with regard to these mundane details. And we are on the track of a hare now, who will, I expect, lead us a merry dance before we are able to track her to her lair."

"I think that I have seen one of the minions of your central spider, if I may be permitted to mix our zoölogical metaphors," I remarked to Holmes.

"What do you mean by that?" he asked me.

"The description that the midwife gave us of the man who brought the baby to her corresponds very closely to that of a man whom I observed in London some time ago."

"Indeed? Where and when was this?"

I outlined the events that had taken place on the afternoon of Bouverie's visit to us, and Holmes sat back, seemingly digesting the news.

"Very good, Watson. Almost certainly Lady Hareby had told your watcher that I had been employed on the case. It is quite likely, I consider, that John Clay, for that is the name of this enterprising young man, to have started keeping his eye on you and me, though whether that is a matter of his own initiative, or whether it has come from his master, I cannot tell. Possibly even Lady Hareby set him on our trail."

"You know him?"

"Our paths have crossed, and I am certain that he is as aware of my existence as I of his, though we have yet to have the pleasure of meeting face to face. His watching you was no accident, of that you may be sure. Mr. John Clay may well be the fourth cleverest man in London, and he is not without a certain nerve and daring. If he is not stopped, he will unfortunately rise high in his chosen career of criminality."

"What are his origins?"

"Rumour has it that he is the by-blow of a Royal Duke. There may well be some truth to that rumour. He undoubtedly possesses connections which are beyond the reach of the common criminal. We must be on our guard when we reach London, it appears."

He lit his pipe and sank into silence.

"I am still unsure with regard to certain details of how you came to discover the baby's existence," I remarked, breaking the silence after about thirty minutes, hoping to draw him out.

"All in good time, Watson. For the nonce, allow me to sit quietly and enjoy the last leisurely smoke I am likely to enjoy for some time. I anticipate the chase to be a troublesome and wearying one."

 N our reaching London, we took a cab directly to Scotland Yard, where we were shown into the office of Inspector Jones, who greeted Holmes with some enthusiasm.

"You have given my men something new to think about," he smiled. "It is not every day that they have the pleasure of following a member of the aristocracy around London."

"I am hoping that she is the minnow who will lead us to the bigger fish," replied Holmes. "Where is she now?"

"My men observed her as she arrived in London, and followed her. She was alone when she stepped off the train, other than for a baby being carried in her arms, and took an ordinary hansom cab to take her to the Darlington family house in Sussex Place."

"Excellent," replied Holmes.

"I am sure that you have your reasons for all of this," went on the Inspector, "and you mentioned in your telegram that this was connected with Lady Hareby's family, but I am unsure exactly what is at stake."

Holmes briefly explained the events of the past few days, and Jones let out a low whistle.

"She sounds like a woman to be reckoned with," he said. "And your goal is to find those who have assisted her?" Holmes nodded in agreement. "In the usual run of things, we would bring her in if we knew as much as you have just told me, but in this case, we will take your advice and work towards the arrest of the whole gang. We have had our eyes on young Mr. Clay for some time, and it will be a positive pleasure to snap the bracelets around his wrists."

"It may take some time before matters develop that far," said Holmes. "In the meantime, Watson and I will return to our rooms. I trust that you will contact me as soon as there are any significant developments?"

"You may depend on that," replied the Scotland Yard detective, and we took our leave of him.

"I am frightened," Holmes suddenly burst out as we were sitting in the cab bearing us to Baker-street.

I stared at him in astonishment. "Surely there is little danger to us here in London from Lady Hareby or those with whom she is in contact?"

Holmes laughed bitterly. "It is not physical danger that I fear. It is the fear of failure. As you know, I am accustomed to success, perhaps more than most men, and as a result the risk of failure sits hard on my shoulders. In this case where we are now engaged, I fear that this may be one of the rare instances where I find myself pitted against forces where even I am unable to prevail. If it were only myself involved, it would not be of great importance, but since I have now let Jones into the secret, anything short of success would be a public failure."

I attempted to cheer my friend, reminding him that success was not to be expected in every instance, and that he should rather remind himself of his triumphs rather than brood upon the possibility of failure, but he appeared unconvinced by my reasoning, and shrank back in his seat, huddled inside his travelling cape. Such a disposition was most unlike Holmes— indeed, I had never before seen him in such a mood as this.

We arrived at Baker-street, where Mrs. Hudson greeted us with the news that we had a visitor waiting outside our rooms, who proved to be a tolerably good-looking young woman, but shabbily dressed, and without any pretensions to gentility.

When Holmes had ushered her into the room, and she was settled into a chair, she began with few preliminaries.

" I want you to bring my baby back," she burst out abruptly. " I should never have sold him."

" You sold your baby?" I asked, somewhat incredulously, sitting forward. Holmes, for his part, continued to lounge in his chair.

" Tell me when and to whom this sale took place," he asked, with seemingly no more emotion that he would have displayed had he been making enquiries about the sale of some vegetables.

" It was just over two weeks ago when he was born," she began, sniffing tearfully. " He was a fine handsome little thing, he was, but I needed the money, so when a gentleman came round and offered me five pounds, I handed over my baby, and got my money."

" What did your husband have to say about this?" I could not help asking, and instantly regretted my words as she looked at me with a bitter smile on her lips.

" You don't need a husband to have babies," she said to me scornfully. " Though some of you lot don't seem to know that."

I reddened, and looked over to Holmes, who appeared to be biting his lips in an effort not to laugh outright, which made me even more angry at my own thoughtlessness. " I apologise," I said at length.

" Can you tell us something of the gentleman who bought your son?" asked Holmes. " What sort of man was he?"

" He wasn't very tall, a bit stout, like. I said he was a gentleman, but I don't think he was a real toff, though he did speak a bit lah-di-dah sometimes. He had the money, though. I saw it when he pulled out his wallet. A whole bundle of five-pound notes. Mind you, I took my money in sovereigns. You know where you are with them."

"Quite right," nodded Holmes. "Banknotes can be troublesome things. Anything else that you can remember about the man?"

"Well, he had this funny mark on him about here," pointing to her own forehead. "It looked a little as if someone had splashed some white paint over him."

"Did you by any chance notice his ears?" asked Holmes.

"It's strange that you should mention that, because I did get a good look at them when he bent down to see the baby. He had holes in them for earrings, but no earrings."

"That is most helpful," said Holmes, casually. "There cannot be too many men in London with those characteristics." I knew from past experience that this relaxed mode of speech and languid attitude usually signified great internal mental excitement on Holmes' part. "Where did the sale take place? Did you visit him, or he come to you?"

"I heard from a friend that there was someone looking for a baby, and I went to this house in Finsbury Park."

"Do you have the address, and also the name and address of the friend who told you about this man?"

She provided the requested details promptly and clearly. "Very good," said Holmes. "I will look into it. I have an interest in this case, so there will be no fee charged."

"Oh, thank you, sir," she replied. "I was worried if five shillings would have been enough."

"I do, however, require your name and address, of course, so that I can report back to you on the progress of the search."

"My name is Mary Brown. I can be reached through the Rose and Crown on the corner of Church-street in Stoke Newington. Talk to Alfred, the landlord there, and he will tell you where I am."

"For the moment I will take your word for it that your

name is indeed Mary Brown," replied Holmes. "However, I would advise you to give your real name to the police, should that become necessary."

"The police?" she asked in some anguish. "You are not a policeman, though?"

"I am not, but what you have just told me leads me to believe that there is a connection to a group of criminals whom I am anxious to apprehend. If it becomes necessary for you to speak to the police, rest assured that I will use the influence I have with them, which I can assure you is not inconsiderable, to save you from any trouble."

It was doubtful whether the young woman fully understood what was being asked of her, but she nodded thoughtfully.

"Very good," said Holmes. "I will be in contact with you soon, never fear."

Chapter XIII
John Clay

E is in my sights, Watson!" Holmes exclaimed excitedly as we were left alone in the room. "The Finsbury Park address we have just been given will surely lead me to him."

As always when he was hot on the trail, Sherlock Holmes was heedless of any possible fatigue and hunger. Though this sometimes left me struggling in his wake, often, as in this case, the thrill of the chase prevented these from being more than minor inconveniences.

"We know that at least one of the parties involved here carries a pistol," he reminded me, as I slipped on my overcoat. "It would seem advisable for us to do the same. I trust we will not need them, but it will be as well to be prepared for any eventuality." Accordingly, both he and I provided ourselves with revolvers, which we slipped into our overcoat pockets.

Before we hailed a cab to convey us to Finchley, Holmes dispatched a telegram to Inspector Jones at Scotland Yard.

"I feel that this is the time to bring him into the game," he said to me. "I am now confident enough of the success of this case to let him have the glory associated with the arrest."

On arrival at the address we had been given by the young mother, which proved to be one of a row of tall terraced houses, backing onto the railway line, Holmes looked about him.

"I see no sign of Jones and his men," said Holmes. "No matter. I am confident that they will be with us soon." He strode up and beat a brisk tattoo on the door-knocker. A smartly dressed maid opened the door to us.

"Good afternoon," Holmes addressed her. "I would like to speak to Mr. John Clay, if he is at home."

The maid's face was a mask of puzzlement. "There's no Mr. Clay at this house, sir," she answered him. There was no doubt in my mind that she was telling the truth, and she genuinely had no knowledge of John Clay.

"Very good," said Holmes. "He is presumably residing here under an alias. I would like to speak with the master of the house."

Again the maid seemed confused. "I think you have the wrong house, sir. There is no master here. Just my mistress."

At that moment, a voice came from the inside of the house. "Who is it, Ann?" The tone and expression seemed familiar, and all at once I recognised it as that of Lady Hareby. I saw from the expression on Holmes' face that he had recognised the voice.

Answering for the maid, Holmes gave his name in ringing tones.

"Show him in, Ann," came the instruction from the interior of the house.

"This way, if you would," the maid addressed us both. We were shown into a richly appointed chamber, somewhat at odds with the rather mean exterior of the house. Lady Hareby was sitting in a chair by the window.

"I believe you were looking for John Clay," she addressed Holmes. Her tone was mocking, but the light from the window behind her made it impossible to see the expression on her face. "I regret to inform you that he is not here."

"Obviously this is not his house, then," remarked Holmes. "The taste in the furnishings of this room would appear to be yours, rather than that of John Clay."

"You are correct, Mr. Holmes. This row of houses belongs to the family of my late husband. I have reserved the use of this house for my own purposes, when I wish to entertain those visitors of whom the family into which I married might not altogether approve, and for purposes such as the one about which you were informed earlier today by the young woman who visited you."

Holmes appeared to take this in his stride. "May I ask how you know about what I have been informed and by whom?"

Lady Hareby laughed unpleasantly. "My dear man," she replied. "I know all the details of which you were informed and who informed you of them, because I sent her to you and told her what to tell you."

I was flabbergasted by this news, but it appeared to be no revelation to Holmes, who merely asked calmly, "Of course, she was not the mother of the child taken to Hareby by John Clay?"

"Of course not. Clay claimed the child from an orphanage somewhere and then went up to Hareby with it. I do not know how and where he arranged the matter. That was his business, not mine. He was well paid for his services, and that is all that concerns me. That child is now accepted as the heir to Hareby Hall and all the estate, and when the old fool dies, it will effectively be mine."

"You know, of course, that you face criminal charges on a number of counts?"

"That is possible, I suppose, if you leave this house alive and manage to inform the police of your suspicions," she replied. As she spoke these words, she produced a pistol from under the cushion against which she had been leaning, and pointed it at Holmes' heart. "And your friend the doctor will not escape me either," she went on. "You should know that I have always been reported to be a very fine shot with firearms. You are, of course, welcome to test whether these reports have any truth to them."

Holmes merely smiled in return. "Eliminating Watson and myself would hardly lead to your inheritance of the estate. It might be somewhat awkward for you to explain our corpses here."

"Clay will dispose of the evidence, and no-one will be any the wiser. Even if I were suspected, it would ensure that I died a free woman. I have friends on the Continent, in countries where the London police have no power."

"I am afraid you are mistaken about the idea that you will not be suspected. I called the police to this place before we left Baker-street. They will be here at any moment, and assaulting Watson and myself would merely add to the list of charges to be read out at your trial."

Her eyes blazed fury. "You have not done this?" she spat at Holmes. "Has he?" appealing to me. "I beseech you to tell me the truth."

"I cannot lie to you," I told her. "With my own eyes I saw him dispatch the message to Scotland Yard."

"Then all is lost!" she wailed, and the pistol wavered in her hand. "I had counted on your egotism, Mr. Holmes, and your self-love. I had anticipated that you would wish to claim all the glory for yourself, and leave none for the police, so you would come alone, or maybe with the bashful doctor here, allowing me to remove the obstacles to my inheritance."

She flung the pistol down to the ground, and dashed to the door, wrenching it open. I started to stop her, but Holmes held my arm in a vice-like grip. "Let her go," he said to me in a hoarse voice. "Whatever happens, it will be for the best."

We heard the door at the back of the house open and slam shut, and Holmes released his grip on my arm. "Wait, and listen," he said, his voice more gentle.

The sound of a train approaching along the railway line at the back of the house grew louder, suddenly punctuated by the noise of the locomotive's whistle and the squeal of its brakes.

"What—?" I asked, but Holmes had already left the room. I followed him out of the back door of the house, into the garden overlooking the railway line a short distance below, from where we could see the driver of the train and his fireman lift the broken bloody figure from the tracks.

We turned away, and re-entered the house, coming face to face with Inspector Athelney Jones and his men, who had made their way through the front door.

" She has gone to meet a higher Justice than we know of on this earth," Holmes said simply.

At that moment, the noise of a baby's crying could be heard, emanating from the upper storey of the house.

 FEW days after the events above, I was able to talk to Holmes about the case for the first time. The demands of my patients, and his discussions with the police about the Darlington case, as well as one on which he was involved on behalf of the Foreign Office, had prevented us from discussing the Darlington case in any detail.

Truth to tell, the ending which Lady Hareby had chosen for herself still haunted my dreams, and I was not anxious to re-live those moments, even through the medium of conversation with my friend.

In the later afternoon, he and I sat down with our pipes, re-maining in companionable silence for at least one half of an hour.

At length, I asked Holmes, " You have explained to my sat-isfaction how the missing Mace was discovered. How did you discover the secret of the child ? "

Holmes knocked out his pipe carefully, saving the dottle for the first pipe of the next day, and refilled it. At last he spoke. " It was obvious, was it not, that there was nothing of the uncanny there ? I think that you and I will both agree that the supernatural can be eliminated. I was therefore forced to concentrate on possible natural causes for these disturbanc-es. What sounds, I asked myself, resemble a baby's crying? We know that a cat's cries may sometimes be reminiscent of those of a baby. But we were told early on by the Earl in our first meeting, if you recall, that the late Lord Hareby had giv-en orders for all the stable cats to be destroyed, as a result of his superstitious nature, and Lady Hareby also denied the existence of any such animal in and around the Hall.

"Added to which, you will remember, the cries were often heard in the daytime, while caterwauling is almost invariably confined to the night hours. I was therefore forced to conclude that the cries were not that of a cat. There are indeed certain large birds of prey that may produce similar noises, as well as birds, such as magpies and jays, capable of imitating human sounds, but the frequent nature of the sounds, again coupled with the fact that they were discerned at all hours, led me to believe that they were not produced by birds.

"Accordingly, I came to the conclusion that there was a young child somewhere in the house, the presence of which was unknown to many members of the household. Three questions then presented themselves to me. The first was whose child it might be. The second, why it was hidden away in secret. The third, where it had been hidden.

"The first question was relatively easy to answer. There was only one woman in the house who had been reported as having been with child recently and that, of course, was Lady Hareby. However, her child was supposedly in the nursery, in plain view, and that led me to my next conclusion. Either she had been delivered of twins, and one of the babies was for some reason hidden, or, which I judged most likely, another baby had been brought in and substituted for the one to which she had given birth. Enough maternal instinct remained in her, however, for her to wish to keep the child close to her when it was born, and she accordingly made her plans. Somehow she had discovered the existence of the priest's hole, probably through her husband, though we will never be sure of this. It may well be that Hareby Hall contains many such secrets, including the entry into the cabinet that I discovered, and that she became possessed of all of these.

"I was therefore sure that Lady Hareby's child was

somewhere in Hareby Hall, in the building itself. It was a hazardous business for her, to be sure, but with an invalid husband, and a father-in-law who found it difficult to climb stairs and who had the additional advantage of being somewhat hard of hearing, it may not have posed quite the danger of discovery that one might initially assume.

"A house of the period of Hareby Hall might well be assumed to have secret hiding places, especially given the history of the region's nobility who held out against the Reformation either openly or covertly. Once Lady Hareby appeared as if by a miracle, apparently from a solid wall, it was clear that the priest's hole that I suspected to exist had an entrance from that part of the house. You saw me pace out the length of the corridor on that floor, and that on the floor above. The corridor connecting the servants' rooms on the floor above was appreciably shorter than that below. While you and Lord Darlington were at luncheon together in the library, I slipped outside and examined the exterior of the Hall. I discovered that part of the Hall on that upper floor was 'blind', in that there were no windows. From one angle, though, it was possible to see a skylight let into the roof, which argued a hidden chamber to me.

"It is always more amusing to let perpetrators reveal their secrets themselves than it is for me to reveal them, and I laid my plans accordingly. I gave the lad Robbins his instructions, which were to take a bucket of wet straw to the room end of the corridor where I was sure the priest's hole was located, and to set light to it when he saw the group assembled around the well for the Ritual of the Mace, after first ensuring that Lady Hareby was present. There was no danger to the Hall, of course, but a sufficient quantity of smoke was produced to give the impression that a fire had broken out in that part of the house where I judged the infant to be hidden.

"As you know, a woman's first instinct when faced with a

fire is to rush to the object she values most, and attempt to
save it. And so it proved in this instance. Despite her many
serious faults, Elizabeth Hareby proved a loving mother to her
daughter, and rushed to save her without prior consideration
of the consequences. When she discovered the trick that I had
played on her, she became angry at the deception, with the results that we observed."

"That was hardly to be wondered at," I remarked.

"Indeed so. In any event, now you see my train of reasoning that led to the discovery of the child."

"Astonishing," I exclaimed.

Holmes waved his hand. "Elementary. The facts of the
matter were there for all to see."

"Has any word of this leaked out? I have seen nothing in
the newspapers regarding this business."

"I am sorry to say that the rumours are already starting to
fly. Lady Hareby's death, despite attempts to portray it as an
accident, is already being accounted a suicide, though none of
the reasons being ascribed approach the truth. There is another rumour, based on truth, and I have no idea of its origin,
that the boy at Hareby is a changeling. It may be some time
before Lord Darlington feels he can show his face in public.
The tongues of rumour are even implicating him in his son's
death."

"How vile!" I exclaimed.

"He is in some ways guilty of neglect of his paternal duties
and failing to control his daughter-in-law," mused Holmes,
"and those rumours may be said to be not altogether without
some foundation."

"And what of the child—I should say the children—now?"
I asked.

"Their future is in some doubt. The girl is currently being
cared for by a nurse appointed by the police. The nurse who
had been employed by Lady Hareby at Finchley Park has been

taken into custody as an accomplice. In the end, I am sure that Lord Darlington will take in the child and accept her as a member of his family. She is, after all, his son's child, at least nominally.

"As to the boy, his future is less certain. It may well be that since it will prove impossible to trace any relatives, he will be cared for in the Darlington household, though whether as a member of the family or not, I cannot say. The fact that there are rumours and scandal spreading already about his substitution for another may well prevent his being fully accepted as a member of the family."

"Poor child," I commented. "It hardly seems like a good start to his life. I trust that he will find a loving home, no matter what society determines to be his final station in this world. I trust to Lord Darlington's good nature in this, though." A thought struck me regarding another aspect of the case which, as far as I was aware, had yet to be satisfactorily resolved. "Has there been any news of the jewellery that stolen from the cabinet when Lady Hareby took the Mace?"

"The police searched the Finchley Park house in which we found her, and discovered some of the Darlington jewellery in the room she was using as a dressing-room. Together with the jewellery was a list of the prices she had obtained for the missing pieces, which had been disposed of through the agency of John Clay."

"Clay again!" I exclaimed.

"Yes, he appears to be a running thread throughout this story. Elizabeth Hareby seems to have been most meticulous in keeping financial records relating to her misdeeds, and this quality has allowed us to discover a little more of her actions. There is a record of the money she paid to Clay to procure the infant and deliver him to Hareby, and the money paid to both the midwife and the nurse for her daughter there as well as the expenses involved in the upkeep of the Finchley Park house."

"And do you think that when I saw Clay in the Park that day, that was coincidence?"

"Almost certainly that was another of Lady Hareby's machinations. Consider. She knew that I had discovered the Mace, and that she was now in my power. She had no reason to be friendly towards me, and she would want to know of my movements, and also yours, given that you had previously visited Hareby Hall without me. Since it was necessary for her to be at Hareby, and for various other reasons, including her condition, it was necessary for her to give this task to another. And who better than Clay, who was already in her service? Naturally she knew that Bouverie was in London on that day, and it is more than likely that she believed him to have consulted me, as indeed he did."

"What of those you believe are controlling Clay?" I asked.

Holmes shook his head sadly. "Without being able to lay my hands on Clay, and without Lady Hareby to guide me in that, I am unable to proceed further with this side of the investigation. It pains me greatly to admit it, but I have to confess failure in this regard, as I must also admit a failure to protect poor Lord Hareby's life."

"Given the mental shock that nearly killed him a month before his death, I would be surprised if he had lived for very much longer."

"But the manner of his death, Watson. I should have been able to prevent it." From my past experience, I knew that it was useless to argue with Holmes when he was in this mood, and accordingly held my peace.

We sat in silence for a while longer, Holmes finishing his pipe, and I had not the heart to disturb him. After a while, I picked up the newspaper and started to read it, while Holmes lounged back in his chair, motionless, other than the movement of his pipe to and from his lips, apparently lost in thought. He surprised me after about twenty minutes of this melancholy stillness by leaping to his feet and exclaiming, " But no matter, Watson. Let us to Alberti's. Or rather, given the very English nature of the case that has just ended, Simpson's, if that is agreeable to you ? "

I assented, and we made our way to the Strand, where we were soon seated, and ordered for ourselves the famous roast beef that is associated with that establishment. As I was spooning the horseradish onto the side of my plate, a thought struck me.

" Did the police ever discover the nature of the poison that was introduced to Lord Hareby's tonic by his wife that nearly caused his death ? "

" I gave the bottle to the Metropolitan Police laboratory, but as you might expect, they are baffled by its nature. It would appear that it is some kind of venom extracted from a South Sea fish. I discovered a reference to such a poison in an account of Malay aboriginals, who have used something similar in their tribal wars. I would surmise that Lady Hareby obtained it as one of the fruits of one of her special friendships, quite probably the affair that she carried on with the Harley Street specialist."

" And that," I added with not a little feeling, " is the same poison that you caused me to ingest at that luncheon with Lord Hareby."

" My dear fellow," replied Holmes. " There was nothing in that horseradish at Hareby that should not have been there. I know this, because I questioned the cook closely, who had prepared it herself, witnessed by the kitchen-maids. I am satisfied that the ingredients that went into that relish were all as they should have been."

" Then what...? "

" The power of suggestion, my dear Watson. Your mind was prepared for the worst, and your body accepted your mind's suggestion. You scoffed at the placebos prepared by Dr. Brendell, but you reacted to my placebo, did you not?"

I was speechless for a moment, and then started to laugh. "I am relieved to hear it," I said, "but why did you do it?"

"I had to bring home to Lord Darlington the fact that he was in danger. You had seen the effects of the poison on his son, and were therefore more susceptible to my suggestion in that regard."

"I see, and I am delighted to hear that I was never in danger, but I beg you not to attempt anything similar in the future."

"Have no fear, my trusty Watson," replied Sherlock Holmes. "It will not happen again." He took a pull at his wine, and continued. "This case, although a failure in some respects, has taught me one or two lessons, the chief of which is never to underestimate the power of a woman determined upon evil. Never again will I consider women as the weaker sex."

That seemed to be his epitaph on the affair, and our conversation passed by mutual consent to other matters.

IF YOU ENJOYED THIS BOOK...

Thank you for reading this story – I hope you enjoyed it.

It would be highly appreciated if you left a review or rating online somewhere.

You may also enjoy some of my other books, which are available from the usual outlets.

ALSO BY HUGH ASHTON

SHERLOCK HOLMES TITLES

Tales from the Deed Box of John H. Watson M.D.

More from the Deed Box of John H. Watson M.D.

Secrets from the Deed Box of John H. Watson MD

The Case of the Trepoff Murder

Notes from the Dispatch-Box of John H. Watson M.D.

Further Notes from the Dispatch-Box of John H. Watson M.D.

The Reigate Poisoning Case: Concluded

The Death of Cardinal Tosca

Without My Boswell

1894

Some Singular Cases of Mr. Sherlock Holmes

The Adventure of Vanaprastha

GENERAL TITLES

Tales of Old Japanese

The Untime

The Untime Revisited

Balance of Powers

Leo's Luck

Beneath Gray Skies

Red Wheels Turning

At the Sharpe End

Angels Unawares

The Persian Dagger (with M.Lowe)

TITLES FOR CHILDREN

Sherlock Ferret and the Missing Necklace

Sherlock Ferret and the Multiplying Masterpieces

Sherlock Ferret and the Poisoned Pond

Sherlock Ferret and the Phantom Photographer

The Adventures of Sherlock Ferret

ABOUT THE AUTHOR

UGH Ashton was born in the United Kingdom, and moved to Japan in 1988, where he lived until a return to the UK in 2016.

He is best known for his Sherlock Holmes stories, which have been hailed as some of the most authentic pastiches on the market, and have received favourable reviews from Sherlockians and non-Sherlockians alike.

He currently divides his time between the historic cities of Lichfield, and Kamakura, a little to the south of Yokohama, with his wife, Yoshiko.

More about Hugh Ashton and his books may be found at: hughashtonbooks.info